STRANGER WITH A GUN

Center Point
Large Print

Also by Bliss Lomax and available from Center Point Large Print:

The Law Busters
It Happened at Thunder River

STRANGER WITH A GUN

BLISS LOMAX

CENTER POINT LARGE PRINT
THORNDIKE, MAINE

TO THE REAL JAMIE

This Center Point Large Print edition
is published in the year 2025 by arrangement with
Golden West Inc.

Copyright © 1957 by Bliss Lomax.

All rights reserved.

The text of this Large Print edition is unabridged.
In other aspects, this book may vary
from the original edition.
Printed in the United States of America
on permanent paper sourced using
environmentally responsible foresting methods.
Set in 16-point Times New Roman type.

ISBN: 979-8-89164-608-7

The Library of Congress has cataloged this record
under Library of Congress Control Number: 2025934462

1

There was nothing permanent about the little settlement that in four years had grown up around Jeptha Wright's general store on the North Fork of the Canadian, in what is now Oklahoma. These were Indian Lands, so designated by the U. S. government and assigned by treaty to the Five Civilized Tribes. Aware that the scratch of a pen in faraway Washington was all that was needed to terminate its existence, Jep Wright had not bothered to give the place a name, his own for instance, and it was known simply as Canadian Crossing.

But four years is a long time, and since the leases which the federal government negotiated for its Indian wards, permitting upwards of a hundred thousand head of longhorn cattle to graze on a lush empire of grass, had been renewed from year to year without question, old Jep and his customers, Texans to a man, were not unduly troubled about the future.

After a long wait of twenty years, they had a Democrat in the White House now. They took additional comfort from it, being Democrats themselves, and their confidence was rewarded almost at once by the establishment of a U. S. post office. Jep cleared out a corner of his store, divided a wooden box into pigeon holes. When it was nailed to the wall, he was in business as Canadian Crossing's first postmaster.

His new responsibilities had a marked effect on Jeptha Wright. He was a shrewd, if ignorant, man with an elastic conscience. He was well acquainted with the law that made it a criminal offense to sell whisky on Indian Lands. He violated it every day and thought nothing of it. He had no intention of foregoing that lucrative end of his business, now that he was a government agent, but he took on a new importance in his own eyes. He had a postal map and in the days he had to wait for the first mail to arrive no one entered the store without being shown the route the mail was to take from Fort Smith, Arkansas.

"It's comin' right up the Canadian," Jep pointed out with a dirty finger nail, "to Turkey Crick and then up to Fort Reno and here. Bi-weekly service they calls it. That means we git mail once every two weeks. I don't know what the first batch will be, but I told this gov'ment man to see we got some newspapers if nuthin' else. Be a big day around here when she comes."

They talked about it in the store and outside under the big cottonwood. It was already May and the days were getting warm. The redbud was in bloom and on the rolling hills the live oaks were a glossy green. Out on the range, when men met by chance, they had something new to talk about; the mail was coming to Canadian Crossing. Few indeed had any reason to believe that there would be anything for them. But they found it an excuse for riding into the Crossing. A score were on hand when the canvas-topped mail wagon arrived. The sack contained only half a dozen letters and several copies of the Fort Smith *Democrat.* But the crowd was not disappointed; it was a beginning.

"Boys, the drinks are on the house," Jep announced. "We gotta celebrate. Jest follow me to the back of the store."

"Wait a minute," one of the group called out peremptorily. "Listen to this."

He had seized one of the newspapers and his eye caught an item on the front page that erased the habitually arrogant smile from his handsome face as he read it.

"It's date-lined Washington, D. C., May 7th . . . five days ago. 'Representative Hubert Rich, Democrat, New Jersey, has introduced a bill in the House to terminate forthwith all stockmen's leases on rangelands in the Indian territory. Congressman Rich charges that the leases were entered into at the behest of certain chiefs, who have profited thereby, but do not represent the will of the great majority of the Indians whose lands are being exploited. His bill cites many abuses the Indians are suffering through the proximity of white stockmen, chiefly the open selling of whisky and the debauching of Indian women. He says he has enough support for his measure to get it out of committee to the floor.' "

Worth Arnett, the speaker, finished reading the article in a charged silence and his glance ran over the ring of fellow Texans who surrounded him. He was younger than most of those in the store, but he had been making a name for himself as a successful stockman. He had started with little or nothing. After four years, he had a herd of five thousand cattle wearing his brand. The arrogance that showed in his smile was reflected in the airs he gave himself and a fiery insistence on getting his rights, and often a little bit more. If he wasn't generally disliked, it was also true that he wasn't popular. But he was young, some said, trying to excuse his swaggering belligerency, and would fine down when he got older. Even his friends could not deny that he was a vain man, and with some reason, for he was tall and lean, even for a Texan. His wavy black hair curled about his ears and his intelligent blue eyes had a searching directness.

"What do you make of it, Worth?" asked Jesse Buckmaster, a bearded, veteran stockman and old enough to be the other's father. He had a small herd, small compared with what some outfits were ranging on these Indian Lands.

"I'm not going to let it throw me, Jesse. A pack of damned fools back East who never saw an

Indian are doing all this agitating. We've heard it before and nothing has come of it. If this bill passes, Cleveland will veto it. He knows where the votes came from that elected him—Texas and the South, I mean."

Of those who heard him, only Jep Wright shared his optimism.

"Worth's got it sized up right," he declared. "We been here too long to be kicked out now. I wouldn't worry about it. We got a couple good Texans in the U. S. Senate. One of 'em owns a half interest in the big 44 outfit. If you boys have to clear out, so will they." Jep chuckled at the thought. "Old Pat will see that don't happen."

Whisky restored their confidence. When they began to drift out, an hour later, Arnett rode a short distance with Buckmaster. The latter had little to say. He was troubled by the story in the *Democrat* and he wasn't of a mind to conceal it.

"You're as gloomy as an owl, Jesse," Arnett chided. "You're taking this too much to heart."

"That's all right for you to say, Worth, you're a young man. I had the ground cut out from under me more'n once when I was your age. I always managed to land on my feet. It's different now. If I was to be ordered out of the Territory, I don't know what I'd do. There's no goin' back to the Texas Panhandle, no open range there. There's no place a man with cattle could turn to, short of Montana, a thousand miles away."

Buckmaster shook his head soberly.

"It ain't only myself I got to think about; there's the girl. It ain't like Jamie was a boy, able to shift for herself."

"She may be a girl," Arnett remarked, with a conceding grin, "but I notice she knows how to handle herself. You needn't worry about Jamie. By the way, how is she, Jesse?"

"Oh, fine, fine. She's been a mite sassy lately. That comes of the way I raised her, I reckon. She gave one of my punchers a dressin' down the other day, I'm tellin' you. When she gits on her ear she uses language you don't find in no dictionary."

"I know," the other acknowledged with a wry smile. "She's given me a sample or two. You tell her I'll be over to see her, first chance I get."

"That'll be all right with me," Buckmaster answered, a definite reservation in his tone. "I can't speak for Jamie, she has ideas of her own."

"Meaning what?" Arnett inquired with a faint hostility. It wasn't only Jamie he wanted; he meant to have the Buckmaster outfit as well. He figured it wouldn't take long; Jesse was old; if that didn't suffice, there'd be other ways. He hadn't got where he was by hard work alone.

Jesse Buckmaster had opened the draw string of a small cotton sack and exposed a piece of Black Strap plug tobacco. He bit off a comfortable chew and made Arnett wait for his answer while he rolled the cud around in his mouth a few times.

"Wal," he drawled thoughtfully, "mebbe it ain't for me to say. But you been buzzin' Jamie for five, six months. I wonder, Worth, if it ain't occurred to you that you may be wastin' your time."

"No, I don't figure it that way," Arnett laughed. "A woman never knows her own mind till a man makes it up for her. You understand my intentions are honorable, Jesse."

"Yes," Buckmaster nodded. "Jamie would see to it that they was." His tone changed abruptly. "Don't you say anythin' to her about this stuff in the paper. I don't intend to mention it and set her worryin'."

They came to where their trails divided. Buckmaster scratched his bay gelding with the spurs and loped away. He still had thirty miles of riding to do. The sun was gone from the sky and the hush of twilight was settling down over the rolling plains when he caught his first glimpse of the cabins of blackjack logs that he had built in a bend of Ten Mile Creek. He had a three-man crew riding for him. Honey Williams, an ancient Negro, who had been in his employ for years, did the cooking.

Though Jesse Buckmaster's years were many, he was a tough-fibered man and in the saddle every day. Usually Jamie rode with him. By the hard standards with which he judged life, he

11

counted her the equal of the best man in his little outfit. She could ride and rope with the best, and she had the tireless energy and tenacity that had kept him going through hard times and good. He knew she had more than that running for her; she had judgment and the unwavering strength of her convictions, something that he had not always had. He was more prosperous now than he had ever been. For years he had wandered back and forth across the Panhandle with his rag-tag outfit, fighting for a little grass, his peripatetic ranch home a covered wagon. Jamie, only a child when her frontier mother died, had shared the wagon with him. She was twenty now. For eight years she had lived on the range among men. The life had sharpened her wits and hardened her mentally and physically.

Jesse had said he didn't intend to say anything about the news that had reached the Crossing, but his preoccupation betrayed him and he had not been at the supper table more than a minute or two before Jamie got the truth out of him.

They ate with the crew. Honey's color did not rule him out. Usually they were half-finished before he brought his plate to the table. It was so this evening.

"You had no reason to hold it back, Dad," Jamie said without reproof. "We've had bad news before and managed to face up to it."

"I know," he grunted. "I didn't want to upset

you. I told Worth I wasn't goin' to say nuthin'."

Jamie's head went up an inch or two.

"I suppose he was able to tell the rest of you exactly what to do." Her voice was rich with sarcasm.

Young Johnny Gaines and Lin Runnels looked up from their plates and grinned. Ike Jarvis, the old man of the crew, expressed his opinion of Worth Arnett with a snort of contempt.

"Just what did he have to say?" she pursued.

"He claims there's nuthin' to it. Says it's jest the work of some cranks back East. He mentioned Pat Jennings. The Senator's got cattle grazin' here. It ain't likely, he argues, that old Pat is goin' to let this bill pass. If it does, he'll git the President to veto it."

"I'm surprised he ain't goin' East himself to tell Mr. Cleveland what to do about it," old Ike observed scurrilously. "If you want my opinion, Jesse, I say it's sunthin' to watch. There's usually fire where there's smoke. If you find you have to go, don't be the last to git started. There's a lot of cattle in this country. There'll be hell to pay if they all hit the trail to somewheres, lookin' for new range, at the same time."

"I agree with you, Ike," said Jamie. "I don't know where we'd head for, but we'd never get there if we waited for the stampede to begin. The big outfits would run us into the ground."

"They'd all be pointin' north, for sure," Johnny

Gaines spoke up. He was a freckled, red-headed man with a perpetually dusty look. He had proven his loyalty to Jamie and her father on more than one occasion. "It'd boil down to a case of Montana or bust. It's a thousand miles, they say, but Texas cattle have been driven that far north." He turned to Buckmaster. "You know about the drive that started 'way down in the Neuces country, eight, nine years ago."

"Yeh, I know about it, Johnny. Old Jim Ferguson was the trail boss. He knew the country and got the herd through. But they had a big losin'—fifteen to twenty per cent, some of it to Injuns."

"But they got through." Jamie Buckmaster's dark eyes warmed optimistically.

She was not pretty in the way of city-bred girls, who went to great length to guard their peach bloom complexions against the ravages of the sun. Her face was deeply tanned and untouched by cosmetics. Her mouth was too strong for mere prettiness. But she had a good nose and forehead. Her dark brown eyes were her best feature. Her chestnut-colored hair had a copperish sheen and deserved more attention than she gave it. It was something less tangible than her looks, however, that was her greatest charm. It was a quality in her voice, in her laughter and the way she carried herself, and most of all in the vitality and zest for life that flowed out of her eyes. She was as slim as a boy, but she had a good figure. In her tight-fitting jeans, faded from washing, and her man-tailored shirt, of Shantung silk, or woolen, depending on the season, there was a witchery about her that had caught the attention of others than Worth Arnett.

"Dad, if we had to, could we get through?" she began again. "That was some years ago that Jim Ferguson made his drive. Conditions have changed—"

"They have. I wouldn't say for the better. There's bob wire in Kansas and Nebraska now. That's a dang sight worse'n Injuns."

Buckmaster's grizzled face grew long as he reflected on those miles to the north. "It would be foolish even to try to git through without a good trail man to lead the way and find water for the stock. I don't know where you'd find one short of Dodge City. And you couldn't be sure even then that you wasn't hirin' a lyin' windbag who'd git you into trouble before you got north of the Kansas line."

The whole subject was painful to him and he wanted to be through with it. With sudden anger, he sent a scowling glance round the table.

"I've heard enough about this for tonight," he grumbled. "Be a couple weeks before we learn which way the wind is blowin'. I'll cross my rivers when I git to 'em."

He had his way about it. If in the days that

followed he refused to listen to any reference to the matter, he could not put it out of his mind. Nor could Jamie. It was far too menacing for that. She had not forgotten the lean years in the Panhandle, living in a wagon, moving hither and yon with their few hundred cows, hoping for little more than to be able to continue their nomadic existence. She shuddered at the thought of going back to such a life. And it could mean that if they were forced out. She knew little about Montana Territory, either good or bad, but it did not loom in her eyes as a Promised Land where, once reached, their troubles would be over. But anything would be preferable to returning to Texas.

In the middle of the week, she and her father came in from the range to find Worth Arnett at the house. She wondered whether he was there just to endeavor to further his cause with her or because he had some news. She could feel him devouring her with his eyes. The attention he had been paying her for some months was not displeasing to her. With his money and good looks, he was widely regarded as quite a catch. It amused her to keep him at arm's length. If she didn't find it difficult it was largely because she had convinced herself that she wasn't interested in him.

"I'll tell Honey you're staying for supper," she said. Ranch courtesy demanded no less. "If you'll excuse me for a few minutes, Worth, I'll go in and freshen up."

Buckmaster was no sooner alone with their visitor than he said:

"You heard anythin' new?"

"Not from Washington. I heard that Nick Brewster had just got home from Wichita, so I went up to the 44 yesterday to have a talk with him. I figured that being the Senator's partner he'd know what was happening, if anyone did. He told me he'd exchanged some telegrams with Pat before he left Wichita."

"How does Pat feel?"

"He says he's confident nothing will come of it. The bill's coming out of committee sure enough, but Pat guaranteed him it would never reach the President's desk. He said something else that doesn't sound too good to me."

"How is that, Worth?"

"The big newspapers back East are hollering their heads off in support of the measure."

"Why in hell don't they mind their own business?" Buckmaster whipped out. "If that goes far enough it could spell trouble."

"Well, if Brewster ain't worried, I don't know why we should be, Jesse . . . You said anything to Jamie?"

"Yeh, she got it out of me. She ain't sayin' much, but I can see it's weighin' on her. When she opens upon you, don't try to put her off. Tell her what you know, and don't sugar-coat it. She'd see through anythin' like that in a minute."

"Leave her to me, Jesse," Arnett said with a smug grin. "I know how to handle her."

"I wonder if you do," Buckmaster grunted to himself as he led the horses down to the corral.

Arnett made himself comfortable on the plank bench beside the door and lit a Pittsburg stogie, a recent innovation in his smoking habits. Jamie found him there when she stepped out. She had brushed her hair with more care than usual and donned a fresh silk shirt. He ran his eyes over her with frank admiration.

"You can do more with yourself in a few minutes than any girl I ever knew," he declared. "And I've known a few."

"I daresay you have, if one can believe the gossip about you," she returned with a disparaging frown. "I want to have a talk with you, Worth. Suppose we walk down to the creek."

"My pleasure," he murmured.

She led him to a spot on the bank that was a favorite with her.

"I know what you're going to ask me, Jamie," he said as they sat down. "I can't say any more than your father has told you. But I'll tell you this: I ain't losing no sleep over this business."

"I wouldn't expect it, you being always so cocksure that everything is going to go your way."

"It usually does," was his grinning, impudent answer.

Without bothering to hide her annoyance with him, she refused to be satisfied until he had given her his version of what had taken place at the Crossing. It added little to what she already knew.

"Is that all you've got to say, Worth?"

"I've given it to you just about word for word," he said with some impatience.

She wasn't through with him.

"It's a long ride from your place up to the 44. You are not in the habit of going there. What were you doing there yesterday afternoon?"

"Who says I was at 44 yesterday?" he demanded irascibly.

"Ike saw you. He was working the brush in the Walnut Bottoms, looking for strays. You went to 44 because you'd heard that Nick Brewster was back, and you wanted to hear how he was taking this trouble. Why don't you admit it?"

"All right, have it your way, Jamie," he gave in throwing up his hands. "I saw Nick. I'll tell you what he had to say."

Her deepening concern was reflected in her young face as she heard him out.

"And you can sit there, Worth, and tell me we've got nothing to worry about—with those Boston and New York and other newspapers clamoring for our scalps?" she demanded indignantly.

"Jamie, it's all politics. They're Republican newspapers. They're out to embarrass the administration. I'm just as anxious as you are to know how it's going to go. But it won't do any good to stew about it. I came over this evening with something else on my mind. There's a dance at the Crossing on Saturday night. I'm inviting you to go with me. I'll come for you. There'll be a full moon. It'll be nice riding home afterwards."

"No, Worth," she said at once, "I wouldn't enjoy myself. I'm in no mood for dancing. I appreciate your asking me, but just take somebody else."

"I'll take you or I'll go alone." He reached out and caught her hand. His eyes were suddenly warm with feeling. "You know I'm serious about you, Jamie."

She looked away, her full lips tightly pressed together and was silent for a moment.

"We've spoken of this before, Worth," she murmured softly. "I'm sorry I can't offer you any encouragement—"

A sudden rush of color touched his tanned, handsome face.

"That's all right, Jamie. You don't think so, but I'm a patient man. I can wait . . . You won't go Saturday night?"

"No—"

• • •

They were at the table, the door open, when a stranger rode into the yard. The excellence of his horse and riding gear, the expensive quality of his clothes, marked him as a man of some importance, at least to himself. It was borne out in the cut of his face, his level gray eyes and the quiet dignity that appeared to rest very easily on him. He got out of the saddle effortlessly and dropping the reins over his horse's head, approached the door.

He was armed. It had no significance; most men wore a gun. But something about the way he wore his, the holster swung a trifle low and a little forward, suggested that he was not inexperienced in its use. Unconsciously he gave his gun-belt a tug to settle it more comfortably on his hips.

"I wonder who he is," Jamie murmured to Arnett, as her father went to the door. "I like his face. He appears to be a man you could trust."

Her interest in the stranger was enough to tip the scales against him in Worth Arnett's mind.

"Chances are he's just another drifter," was his disparaging comment. "From the north, no doubt."

"I'm sorry to bother you," they heard the man at the door say. He had a pleasant voice and his words were unhurried. "I don't know whether I've lost my way or not. Am I going right for Canadian Crossing?"

"Yeh," Jesse told him. "You ain't gone out of your way none. Jest follow this crick about five miles till you come to a big lightnin' killed walnut. Swing off to your right a mile or so and you'll hit a trail that'll take you to the Crossing. It's a piece . . . 'bout thirty-five miles."

"Thank you," the stranger smiled. "I understand I can get accommodations there."

"You can, if you ain't too particular. Jep Wright will put you up." This soft-spoken stranger appealed to him as he did to Jamie. "Supper's on the table, mister. You better come in and eat. I'm Jesse Buckmaster."

He held out his hand. The other pulled off his gloves and they shook hands.

"My name is Kinnard—Frank Kinnard. I'm obliged to you for asking me in. I don't want to intrude."

Jamie noticed how smooth and untanned his hands were. The disturbing thought that they might be the hands of a gambler or a gunman crossed her mind.

Jesse introduced the stranger. After some talk around the table, Arnett said: "You're a northern man, I take it."

"I am," was the quiet response.

"Dodge City?"

Asking a man where he hailed from was a question not usually put to a stranger. Dodge was tough and lawless. Arnett's tone seemed to suggest that that was what he had in mind.

There was a moment's awkward silence. Ike Jarvis cleared his throat nervously. Jamie was watching the stranger. For a fleeting instant his mouth tightened. He smiled then. Beneath its disarming surface her sharp eyes detected something coldly dangerous.

"I am not unacquainted there," Kinnard said softly. "If you are interested, Mr. Arnett, I'm better known in Deadwood and Dakota."

Arnett's handsome face paled with anger, but he turned the challenge with an ironic twist of his lips.

"I'm interested only if you're looking for a job. I could use another man."

Jamie saw the stranger's mouth relax and knew the tension of this moment was gone.

"If it was a job I wanted," Kinnard said easily, "I imagine I could find one nearer my home range."

Arnett subsided and did not address him again. Buckmaster carried the conversation. It was concerned with further directions on the best way to reach Canadian Crossing, the weather and the like.

The stranger ate sparingly. It piqued Jamie that he paid so little attention to her. But an occasional intercepted glance of his gray eyes said that he was making his estimate of her. Her father and the crew went out with Kinnard when he left. Arnett remained at the table with her.

"I got his number," he said, with a supercilious grin. "I'll wager he shipped his trunk ahead of him when he left Deadwood, or wherever it was. He's down here to give some trouble a chance to cool off on his back trail."

"Well," she shrugged enigmatically, "he at least got our minds off our own troubles . . . You know, Worth, I think I've changed my mind about Saturday night. If you'll come for me, I'll go to the dance."

2

A wooden awning, supported by unpeeled locust posts, extended out from the front of Jeptha Wright's general store. There, seated on an upturned box, Kinnard had spent most of his time since arriving in Canadian Crossing. Late in the afternoon, when the sun made the porch uncomfortable, he moved out under the big cottonwood, or inside, talking over the counter with Jep. No one who came to the store, or stopped next door at Ed Hines' blacksmith shop, escaped his attention.

Jep realized almost at once that the stranger, who occupied his only spare room, was waiting and watching for someone. There was always talk in the store, most of it concerned with what was happening in Washington and the likely outcome. The newcomer not only took no part in it but showed plainly enough that the matter was of little interest to him. Jep tried to draw him out. He got nowhere. It became more than his curiosity could stand, and on Saturday morning, as they breakfasted together, he put a question into words that had been troubling him for three days.

"I don't want to pry into your private business, Kinnard," he began haltingly. "As you know, I'm the postmaster here. Kinda makes me a gov'ment man . . . By any chance are you a deputy U. S. Marshal?"

"No, nothing like that, Jep," the other answered, with a smile in his gray eyes. "I'm looking for a party who did me dirt. In fact, I've been trying to run him down for about ten months. He's a Texan, of a sort. I was tipped off that he'd drifted down this way."

"There's all kinds of Texans, same as everythin' else," Jep observed philosophically. "If he's a blackleg, it ain't likely he's a friend of mine . . . You care to name him?"

Kinnard, a little surprised by the old man's sudden directness, put down his cup and pushed back from the table.

"I'm tempted to, Jep," he said quietly. "I got you sized up for a square-shooter. You might be able to help me. I know you got a wide acquaintance."

"Men comin' and goin' all the time, Kinnard. I don't know 'em all."

"Do you know a man named Hank Fordice?"

"A cowpuncher?"

"If he was doing any honest work it would be punching cows."

Jep looked out into the store and made sure they were alone, though the hour was early.

"A smallish man—with a scar through his right eyebrow?"

"That describes him."

Jep nodded to himself, as though confirming a long-held opinion of Fordice.

"No good—never was," said he. "I was acquainted with him years ago, out in the Panhandle. I ain't seen him around here. That don't mean he may not be workin' for some outfit below the river."

"If he's around, he may show up for the dance," Kinnard reflected. "There'll be a crowd—"

"There usually is," Jep agreed. He leaned forward with a troubled glance. "I wouldn't like to have no trouble here tonight, Kinnard. You gunnin' for Hank Fordice?"

"Not if it can be helped. I want to take him back north."

"So?" Old Jep shook his head cynically. "You figger it'll be as easy as that, eh? Hank may have a different idea about it."

"I don't expect him to be too hard to convince," Kinnard said in his detached, impassive way. Getting to his feet, he walked out through the store and took his favorite seat under the wooden awning.

Jep watched him for a moment or two. Grumbling to himself, he began washing the breakfast dishes.

"I never should have taken him in," he reflected. "Soon as I laid eyes on him I knew he spelled trouble. If Fordice happens to show up tonight, there'll be a shootin' as sure as Grant took Richmond."

He considered briefly asking Kinnard to move on. After mulling it over, chewing his mustache the while to ease his mental processes, he decided that it was too late for that. He had nothing against Kinnard. In fact he had come to like him already. But it was not how the stranger might make out that distressed him. It was the shooting itself. For four years men had been bringing their quarrels and bitter antagonisms to Canadian Crossing, but he had proclaimed it neutral ground, and his obstreperous customers, needing a place to trade, had been quick to see an advantage for themselves in regarding it as such. If there had been no shootings, they had been avoided on more than one occasion by the narrowest of margins.

Jep Wright was justifiably proud of that record, feeling that in a way it was a mark of the respect in which he was held. He was loath to see it sullied, but as the day wore on and he moved back and forth about the store, waiting on trade, he had a feeling in his bones that the peace that had never rested too easily on Canadian Crossing would be shattered by gunfire before another sun rose in the sky.

"It ain't Kinnard I'm afraid of," he reflected. "He'll keep his head; it's Fordice. I hope to God he don't show up!"

And yet, somehow, he knew he would. He couldn't explain it. In the afternoon, the sky became overcast. Jep walked out to have a look at it.

"Goin' to rain," he said. "We could git a real sod-soaker."

"That would ruin the dance," Kinnard remarked with some interest.

That was what Jep was hoping.

"We'd have to put it off till next Saturday."

But it proved to be only a shower. The sun licked up the moisture greedily and an hour afterwards there was no sign left that it had rained at all, save for the closeness of the air as the warm, humid evening came on.

Dances were a regular thing at the Crossing. Across the road from the store a wooden platform had been laid on the ground. It was roofed over but left open on all sides, around which ran benches for the onlookers, and for the dancers themselves when they left the floor temporarily. A small dais-like box of unplaned boards at the far end of the "dance parlor" was for the accommodation of the musicians, always at least two and sometimes as many as three fiddlers. Coal-oil flares, attached to the posts that supported the roof, supplied a weird, smoky light.

Jep called Kinnard in to supper earlier than usual. Fried ham, hominy grits and black coffee.

"Nuthin' fancy tonight," he said apologetically. "I'm goin' to be busy this evenin'. Want to git the dishes and ever'thin' out of the way."

He mopped his perspiring face with a red bandana that was none too clean.

"Not a breath of air stirrin'," he complained. He ate in a preoccupied way for several minutes, and then without warning he looked up and gave the man across the kitchen table a darting glance. Apropos of nothing that he had left unfinished, he said, "If Hank Fordice does happen to show up, he may not come alone. You could find yourself in a ruckus that might be a mite too big for you to handle."

"Jep, why don't you come out and say it?" Kinnard said, undeceived by the other's solicitous tone. "You've been hinting at it all day. You'd like for me to pull away from the Crossing—"

"Only for tonight. If Fordice comes, or if he don't, I'll find out where you can locate him and let you know."

"No," Kinnard said flatly, "I'll stick it out. If the dance doesn't bring him, I'll pull up stakes in the morning and drift down into the Panhandle."

Night fell. Fireflies flickered fitfully across the high brush. In the trees, the cicadas began their grinding, scratching, and endless "see saw—saw see." Cal Evans, the blacksmith's apprentice, lit the coal-oil flares across the way. One of the musicians lived in the Crossing. He was on hand early. Presently a second man, carrying a violin case strapped over his shoulder, rode in. The two conferred briefly and then came across the road to the store.

"Reckon there'll be only Joe and me tonight," the second man informed Jep. "Chester fell off a hoss this mornin' and banged up his shoulder. I stopped for him, but he couldn't come."

"I'm sorry to hear about Chester," said Jep. "The two of you is enough; you can keep folks hoppin' till midnight. Better wet your whistles while you're here."

They were agreeable and followed him to the rear of the store. From a barrel of Mountain Dew he filled two tin cups with whisky and handed them across the board.

From as far as fifty miles away men and women, not all of them young, began to arrive for the dance. They came by horseback, buckboard and wagon. Canadian Crossing came to life and throbbed with laughter and excitement. The fiddlers began to tune up. Leaving the ladies to exchange bits of gossip and news with one another, the masculine contingent streaked across the road to the rear of Jep Wright's store to imbibe. This was according to custom. There was talk about the situation in Washington, but they were in a holiday mood and refused to be cast down.

From a corner of the store porch, where the

yellow lamplight from within did not reach him, Kinnard watched them come and go, the glowing end of his cigarette making strange arabesques in the shadows as he raised it to or lowered it from his lips. No less than forty men had come to the Crossing tonight. The one he sought was not among them. His disappointment was tempered by the fact that he had not set his hopes too high.

"It was just a chance," he reflected. "It's still early. Late comers are still showing up."

He saw Jamie Buckmaster arrive with Arnett. She looked different in skirts, but feminine attire could not conceal her boundless energy and vitality. She was prettier than he remembered her from their first meeting. The music was playing. Arnett led her out on the floor at once. He watched them circling about. She danced with a graceful abandon that held the eye. You saw at once that she enjoyed dancing for its own sake; that she lost herself in a sort of unconscious exhilaration.

It got to be nine o'clock. Kinnard gave up any thought of seeing Hank Fordice tonight. Crossing the road, he moved up to the edge of the dance floor and stood there with his back to one of the posts that supported the roof. Jamie whirled by with Arnett. She saw him and smiled a greeting. Worth Arnett saw him too, but he gave no sign of recognition.

The music stopped briefly and the dancers changed partners. A red-headed young man, a cowpuncher by the look of him, captured Jamie. They passed Kinnard a number of times. When the number ended, they stopped almost at his elbow. It wasn't altogether by chance. Jamie introduced him to her partner. He didn't catch the name. It didn't matter. The young man excused himself and followed his friends across the road to Jep's for refreshment.

"Don't you dance, Mr. Kinnard?" she inquired with engaging frankness.

"I do. It's not one of my better accomplishments, I must admit. It's a pleasure to watch you. If you will permit a compliment, Miss Buckmaster, you are the best dancer on the floor."

"It's not deserved, but I thank you," she said prettily.

She told herself again that she liked the sound of his voice. It rested pleasantly on the ear and was a welcome relief from the Texas drawl that she heard every day.

The music struck up.

"If you'll excuse my awkwardness, mam, I'd be honored if you would dance with me."

"I'd be delighted," she smiled.

Before they were half-way around the floor, she glanced up at him and said in mock reproof:

"You are too modest, Mr. Kinnard; you really dance very well—"

"I can't throw myself into it the way you do. I never could."

"Nonsense," she chided. "You know, of course, that every girl here has her eyes on you, wondering who you are and hoping they'll get to dance with you before the evening's over."

"With due respect, mam, I must doubt that," he remarked with becoming humility. "I've been here long enough to discover that a northern man is regarded with some suspicion in Oklahoma."

"You catch us at a bad time. You've heard the talk. You know we may be forced out."

"I haven't heard much else," he acknowledged. "I didn't know anything about this threat to cancel your leases till the other day. I can't say it surprised me . . . Or maybe I shouldn't have said that."

"Why not? You have an opinion. What is it, Mr. Kinnard?"

"No," he demurred, with a shaking of his head, "I prefer not to say. You'd want the truth from me. It might spoil the evening for you."

She did not press him further at the time. When the music stopped and the fiddlers put down their instruments, preparatory to a trip across the road for another helping of Jeptha Wright's Honey Dew, the dancers left the floor to wait out the intermission.

"I'm afraid the benches are all filled, mam," Kinnard said apologetically, after some searching.

"It's just as well," Jamie told him. "We can step out under the trees."

She steered him beyond the edge of the crowd, and as soon as they were alone, she questioned him about his mysterious reluctance to speak frankly.

"You know how serious this matter is for us. If you have any knowledge of what we may expect, I beg you to tell me, Mr. Kinnard, no matter how discouraging it may be."

"If I had any information, mam, I'd be happy to pass it on to you. All I've got is an idea. In the short time I've been here, I haven't heard anyone suggest that there may be more to this move than appears on the surface. I'm sure there is."

"Do you mind explaining?" she asked, with a puzzled frown.

"I mean the real reason for forcing you folks out is not mentioned in the bill that has been introduced in Congress."

"You think you know what it is?"

"I believe I do. I'm convinced that the government is getting ready to move other tribes into this country. There's been pressure to that effect for some time up north. Stockmen's associations have been fighting to get the size of a number of Indian reservations trimmed down. Fort Belknap for one. Disease, mostly smallpox, has carried off so many Assiniboines and Gros Ventres that only a few hundred are left. It's been estimated that each one of them, men and women, has about four thousand acres set aside for him. It is the same in other places. It don't make sense to cowmen who want more range. You've got the Indian Territory, they tell the government. Why not move the smaller tribes down there?"

He paused to light a cigarette. His manner turned sober and more detached, as though his thoughts were suddenly far away.

"They won't touch the Sioux," he went on after a moment. "It'll be tribes like the Northern Cheyennes and the Arapahoes who'll be herded down here. This climate is too warm for them, after what they've been used to for all the years. The poor devils will die like flies. I suppose that'll be all right with the big boys in Washington who run Indian affairs."

Without seeming to, Jamie studied his face in the moonlight filtering down through the trees. She was struck by its sternness.

"You sound so bitter," said she. "This must mean something to you."

"I'm no Indian lover. It's just that I figure they got some rights. I'd like to see them get a square deal for once."

They had reached the road and were strolling back to the crowd when Worth Arnett found them. He was plainly disgruntled at finding them together.

"Worth, you remember Mr. Kinnard," Jamie

said, ignoring the awkwardness of the moment. He jerked an impersonal nod, and she continued. "We were just discussing the move to cancel our leases. He thinks there's an angle to it that we have overlooked."

She acquainted him with what Kinnard had said. He professed to see little merit in it.

"If that were what is behind this business, the politicians would be using it for a talking point. You don't hear a word about it."

"You will—just as soon as the leases are cancelled." Kinnard was aware of the other's hostility. He was profoundly indifferent to it. "You'll hear a lot about the money it will save the taxpayer to close up a number of reservations and move the wards of the nation down here—and how much happier they will be sharing a territory of their own with the Five Tribes." His short laugh was brittle with sarcasm. "They'll hate it, and so will the Five Tribes who'll be done out of your grazing fees."

"You sound so positive you frighten me," Jamie said with frank anxiety. "You don't seem to feel there's a chance we can hold on."

"Not for long, mam. This is only the first gun they're firing. Nothing may come of it. For your sake, I hope so. But they'll have another try at it. It may be six months, maybe a year, before you have to get out. I don't believe you can hope for more than that."

"That's only your opinion, Kinnard," Arnett remarked with ill-concealed contempt. "I don't suppose you really know any more about it than we do."

"As you say, it's only my opinion," Kinnard agreed with an enigmatic smile. "I was asked for it or I wouldn't have given it."

The music had struck up again. Over her shoulder Jamie gave him a smile that was faintly tremulous as she permitted Arnett to lead her away. Braving the latter's displeasure, she said:

"I'll save another dance for you, Mr. Kinnard."

For some time he stood just behind the benches, watching the dancers and studying the crowd. There was gaiety here, more among the men than the women, thanks to frequent visits to Jep Wright's barrel of Mountain Dew, but even with them, now that he examined them more closely, he realized that it was only a surface gaiety; temporarily hidden away in the mind of everyone present was the gnawing fear of what their fate was to be.

At last, Jamie caught his eye, signalling that the next dance was to be his. With bad grace Arnett turned her over to him.

"Worth has a beastly temper," she said, as they whirled off. "There are times when his manners are as bad as his temper."

"Think nothing of it, mam. He has an excellent opinion of himself, perhaps not without reason."

He smiled down at her. "I'm inclined that way myself. . . . He didn't like what I had to say."

"No. He's sure everything is going to be all right. That hasn't been my opinion—not from the first. What you've had to say has convinced me that we're really in trouble."

Suddenly she felt his arm relax and with a quick movement he stopped and pushed her in back of him. Other dancers had stopped. The musicians checked themselves abruptly and put down their fiddles. Something electric ran through the crowd and a hush fell across the dance floor. A tow-headed little man, his hat pushed back on his head, had stepped to the edge of the floor. He had a short, pugnacious nose and a mean pair of eyes. He had been drinking heavily and he swayed slightly as he stood there, rooted in his tracks, his surprise as great as Kinnard's. Though his brain was fogged with alcohol, he knew instantly, and with a terrible certainty, why the other was in Oklahoma. Hatred burned into his eyes and his mouth twisted in an ugly grimace.

They stood that way for second on second, Kinnard, his shoulders rigid and expectant, making not the slightest move; Hank Fordice bent slightly forward and balancing himself on the balls of his feet. In that interval the other couples drew back. Worth Arnett rushed out on the floor and grabbed Jamie. Her face was white beneath its tan.

"I'm getting you out of here before that drunk goes for his gun." Arnett's voice was gruff and violent. "Be quick!"

The thought that held Fordice chained concerned the gun he wore on his hip. It was only inches away from his twitching fingers, but being well acquainted with the man he faced, the distance seemed almost too great. He had only to consider the alternative to have his decision forced on him. Win or lose, he'd make his play here.

"Stop him, Worth!" Jamie cried as the little man fumbled for his gun. "He'll kill someone!"

She knew Arnett was fast with a .45, but with a swiftness that surprised her, he drew and fired. Fordice flung out his arms in a vain attempt to keep his feet as the slug thudded into his heart. He was dead before he crashed to the floor.

The young Texan turned him over with his boot and stood staring down at the lifeless hulk.

"Better him than some innocent party," he said thickly, excusing himself for what he had done. "The damned fool, going for his gun with all these women around!" He gave Kinnard a long, hostile glance. "I ain't excusing your part in it, mister. If you had any reason to suspect you might have trouble with him, you didn't have to wait for it here. You don't deny you knew him?"

"I knew him." Kinnard's answer was grim and tight-lipped. "He's no use to me dead; I wanted to take him back north alive." His face was hard and flat with a rocking anger. "There was no call for you to use your gun on him."

His voice dripping sarcasm, Arnett said:

"That's appreciation for you." He called on the crowd to witness the other's base ingratitude. "He was ready to cut you down."

"He'd have changed his mind if you hadn't lost your head—or I would have changed it for him. It ain't likely that our trails will ever cross again, Arnett, but if they do, I'm warning you now, don't ever take it on yourself to mix in my business."

His talk struck out recklessly, shattering the moment's pin-drop silence. Jamie got in between them.

"Please let this misunderstanding stop where it is," she entreated. "If anyone is to blame it is I, I asked Worth to stop that man, I saw he was drunk. There was no telling what might happen."

"Very well, Miss Buckmaster, I'll say no more about it," Kinnard answered stiffly.

She followed him when he walked away.

"Will you be leaving the Crossing now?"

"Not for a few days. I'm interested in hearing the news from Washington."

She hesitated, trying to frame a question that she found difficult to put into words.

"If the news is bad—if we have to get out immediately—would you consider trail bossing our outfit to Montana? I know you could get us there—"

"I don't know why I should do that, mam. If the news is as bad as that, cattle will go cheap around here. I have some money. I could put a trail outfit together in a hurry. I'd prefer that to hiring out for wages."

With a catch in her voice, she said scathingly:

"I'm disappointed in you, Mr. Kinnard, I didn't believe you were the sort of man who'd wait around to take advantage of our misfortune."

He was slow to answer. When he spoke it was with dignity.

"With due respect, mam, I must resent your remarks. I've been accused of many things, never of preying on the unfortunate. I'll bid you good evening."

3

Hank Fordice was buried without ceremony on the bank of the North Fork, where other good men and bad had found their final resting place. The repercussions to his slaying were slight. Some held that Arnett had acted hastily. Others regarded him as something of a hero. If there was any feeling against the stranger from the north, it was only because he had brought his troubles to the Crossing. All were agreed, however, including Jep Wright, that if Kinnard lingered there long, a violent, head-on clash with Arnett would be unavoidable.

Jep worried about it all morning and when he sat down to dinner with Kinnard at noon, he was ready to speak.

"I can't supply you with bed and board much longer," he said with unvarnished bluntness. "It ain't that I got anythin' agin you; it's jest that I got to think of myself a bit. I know Worth Arnett is a hothead and somethin' of a damned fool, but he's a good customer, and he's got friends. I can't afford to go agin him. Keepin' you under my roof makes it look like I'm sidin' with you."

He drained his cup and refilled it from the pot.

"If I let you stay, there's sure to be more trouble between you—"

"If there is, it'll be of his making," Kinnard said without taking offense. "But I won't embarrass you, Jep. As soon as the next mail arrives and I catch up on the news from the East, I'll hit the trail. While we're talking, Jep, I'd like to ask you a question. Why didn't you let me know Fordice was in here drinking? You could have sent word across the road."

"Why, he never set foot in the store!" the old man cried, banging his heavy cup on the table with an indignant bang. "I never laid eyes on him till after the shootin'. He'd changed some since last I saw him, but I'd have spotted him. I figger he musta jest rode in out of the brush and headed straight for the dance parlor. By the looks of his hoss, he had come a long piece. We went through his saddlebags. He didn't have a bite of grub with him."

"Did he have any money?"

"A little silver, that's all. Spent what he had for whisky along the way, I reckon. If he wasn't runnin', him travelin' light that a-way, I miss my guess."

It was a shrewd surmise and its correctness was proven no later than the following morning, when a young cavalry lieutenant and a detail of four troopers rode into Canadian Crossing and pulled up at Jep's place. The morning was unusually pleasant and it had brought half a dozen people, including Jamie Buckmaster and her father, in for supplies. When Lieutenant MacGruder got down from the saddle and walked into the store, Kinnard got up from his seat under the wooden awning and followed him in.

The military appeared in the Crossing so infrequently that everyone in the store realized at once that only something out of the ordinary could account for their presence there this morning. Lieutenant MacGruder did not keep them waiting for an explanation. A trooper had been robbed and killed by a cowboy belonging to an outfit delivering beef at Fort Gibson. The man's identity was known, and for three days MacGruder and his men had been tracking him down.

"We know he was headed this way," said the lieutenant. "We thought we had him night before last, but he got across the North Fork and gave us the slip."

He gave them a description of the wanted man.

Against her will Jamie flicked a quick glance at Kinnard and he exchanged a knowing nod with Jep. The latter said:

"Reckon I can supply his name, Lieutenant. Hank Fordice?"

"Yes—"

"Then you needn't look any further. He's underground, down on the river bank."

Jep explained the circumstances. Kinnard and

several others confirmed his story. MacGruder made some notes. He was not displeased over the outcome of his mission.

"This will save the government the bother and expense of bringing him to trial," said he. "It's nice when you can return a favor for a favor," he went on, with a rueful smile, "but it doesn't look as though we're going to be able to this time. I'm afraid that when we come back we'll be here to move you out."

Their startled faces told him that he had dropped a bombshell.

"Why, I thought you folks knew—"

"We know only that there's a bill in Congress to cancel our leases," Jamie spoke up, steadying her voice with an effort. "We get mail here now, but only twice a month. It'll be almost a week before we get the next Fort Smith newspapers. Has something been done?"

"Definitely, mam. We get our news from the East by telegraph. We had word just before I left the post that the bill had passed and was on the president's desk."

"No!" Jesse Buckmaster groaned, as though he couldn't believe his ears. "How could they've jammed it through that fast?"

"They attached a rider to the bill calling for the abandonment of a number of northern reservations and shifting the tribes down here. I imagine that's why the bill got so much support.

It sailed through in a hurry. No doubt it's being talked up as a move to save the government money."

Jep Wright, the Buckmasters and the others were stunned for a moment. Jamie turned to Kinnard, her pique forgotten.

"It's happened just as you said it would, Mr. Kinnard," she said, pulling herself together with a visible effort. "President Cleveland will sign the bill, of course."

"I must think so. But whether he does or not is beside the point. When a bill has that much support it can be passed over a veto." For the first time he addressed himself to the lieutenant. "Have you any idea how long these people will be given to get out?"

"Thirty days, I understand."

"Thirty days—thirty days!" Jep cried aghast. "Damn their souls, they ain't givin' a man time enough to git turned around!"

MacGruder and his troopers left the Crossing a few minutes later, but not the others. The little crowd grew as the day wore on. They were too bewildered to do anything but talk and draw some faint measure of security just from being together.

Worth Arnett and one of his men drove up late in the afternoon. He swaggered into the store, big and important. The air of gloom that hung over the place struck him at once.

"Why is everybody wearing a long face?" he demanded with a derisive grin. "You look like a lot of sick sheep."

"Thanks for the compliment, Worth," said Jamie, taking him up at once and letting him feel her annoyance. "Your face may be as long as ours when you've heard the news. We won't have to wait for the next mail. We're going to get thirty days to get off this range."

She and Jep gave him a detailed account of what MacGruder had had to say, and the nature of the business that had brought him to Canadian Crossing. Arnett listened with a cynical grin on his handsome face. His skepticism wasn't as genuine as he pretended, but he had taken a position in this matter and he was determined to maintain it.

"I'll believe that tale when I see it in print, not before," he said flatly. "This MacGruder was just pulling your leg—spouting a lot of nonsense like that and you with your mouths open, ready to swallow it."

"MacGruder knew what he was talking about," old Jep burst out defiantly. Now that he was convinced the jig was up, as far as trade was concerned, he saw no reason for currying favor with the tall Texan. "It don't do no good to look the other way when news is bad and tell yoreself it ain't so. That's jest bein' pig-headed. Tomorrow mornin' I'm goin' to cut prices on everythin' in this store and git rid of the stuff. That's how I feel about it."

Jamie didn't have to remind Arnett of what Kinnard had had to say on the night of the dance; she knew he remembered. She could see it in his eyes as he glared at the stranger. His hatred of the man she could understand. But that wasn't the sum of it; in some obscure way he seemed to hold Kinnard responsible for what was about to happen. It told her plainly enough, no matter what he said to the contrary, that he knew as well as she did that they would have to go.

She was not soon to forget the picture they made as they were facing each other, Arnett hotheaded, reckless, arrogant, and Kinnard completely self-contained, sure of himself. Knowing it needed only a word to whip them to violence, she drew a breath of relief when Arnett turned back to the counter and handed Jeb a list of what he wanted. When the goods were set out, he and his man carried them to the buckboard and drove away at once.

Kinnard wandered out of the store and sat down on the platform. He had been there only a few minutes when the Buckmasters came out. Jamie stopped to speak with him.

"We're going," she said. "It will be late when we reach the creek. I'm sorry I lost my temper with you the other night. In a way, you prepared me for the news we got today. I have to thank you for that." With a movement of her head she indicated her father, who had gone on to the horses. "It's bowled him over. He just couldn't believe it would happen."

She was trying to put on a brave face but as she hesitated momentarily he saw her chin quiver.

"He's worked hard all his life," she continued. "Luck seemed always to be against him till we came here. To be cut down now, when he's doing well, is what makes it twice as hard to bear."

Kinnard nodded sympathetically. He told himself she meant nothing to him, but he couldn't help admiring her courage.

"Give him a little time and he'll be all right. He's fortunate he's got you to lean on, mam. If you're going to have thirty days to get out, that'll mean thirty days after the government has notified you officially."

"There's no telling how soon that will be."

"No, but it'll give you some extra time. Your father can think things out and decide exactly what he wants to do."

Jamie shook her head stoically.

"I'm afraid there's very little left for him to think out, Mr. Kinnard. It means Montana. There's nothing else."

"He can drive his stuff up to one of the railroad towns in Kansas and dispose of it," he reminded her. "You heard one or two say this afternoon that that's what they intend to do—"

"We want to stay in the cattle business, Mr. Kinnard—not get out of it."

Her tone carried a definite rebuke.

Jesse Buckmaster was in the saddle. He called for her to come along. She glanced up at Kinnard, and her dark eyes were touched with a new bleakness.

"I take it you'll be leaving as soon as you can pick up some stock at a bargain."

"It depends. The price will have to be right. If I buy some top-grade longhorns, I know there won't be much left of them, just skin and bones, by the time I get them into the Bad Lands. It's a gamble. I may change my mind."

"Then this may be the last time I'll be seeing you—"

Though she was not aware of it, a little catch came into her voice. He regarded her closely for a long moment. He couldn't understand why she suddenly seemed important to him. To his surprise, he caught himself saying, "I'll manage to see you again, mam, before I go."

She turned in the saddle and raised her hand in a friendly farewell. Kinnard returned it and stood watching until a bend in the trail hid her from view.

"She's much too fine for Arnett," he mused.

The arrival of the bi-weekly mail from Fort Smith not only confirmed Lieutenant MacGruder's story but carried the further information that the Indian Lands Bill had been signed into law.

Jep Wright's store wasn't big enough to accommodate the crowd that had gathered. It flowed out under the wooden awning and the big cottonwood. The news hardly came as a bolt out of the blue, and yet a few, Jesse Buckmaster among them, had dared hope that something would intervene to save them. Now, seeing it in print, they had to believe it. Arnett, as usual, had a lot to say. Most of it was directed at those small owners who, in their panic, were ready to sell their cattle for whatever they would bring. Kinnard had let it be known that he might be interested. Several owners had talked price with him. Arnett knew it, and it was really at Kinnard that he was taking aim.

"All right, give your stuff away if you want to," he stormed. It infuriated him to find so few willing to listen to what he had to say. "That damn Yankee knew this was coming. He's just been waiting to pick your bones clean."

A heavy hand fell on his shoulder and swung him around. He hadn't seen Kinnard step off the platform and join the group gathered under the cottonwood.

The onlookers fell back, expecting both men to reach for their guns. That intention was written plainly enough on Arnett's lean tanned face. But he hesitated, and it seemed to surprise him, as though he didn't quite know why he did.

"You've got a running mouth, Arnett, and a nasty habit of interfering in other people's business," Kinnard said thinly. "If you got anything more to say against me, let's hear it."

Arnett stood there, towering above him, his shoulders rolled forward, swaying with rage. Fear, caution, some mental process, had restrained him a moment before. It had no power over him now. His hand flashed down to his gun. Kinnard had him covered before he got it out of the leather.

The crowd, grown large by now, gasped its astonishment. They were not unfamiliar with the fast draw, but they had never witnessed anything like this before.

"Better forget it, Arnett," Kinnard spoke with a quiet confidence. "I wouldn't like to soil my gun on you. Don't make it necessary."

The tall Texan's hand came away from his gun. It was a cruel, bitter moment for him. His eyes swept the circle of watching men. He found no sympathy for himself in their dark, inscrutable faces. In fact, they were enjoying his discomfiture. And with good reason. In the past, whenever it had served his purpose, he had run roughshod over many of them. This was a time for remembering it. Desperate, he attempted to bluster his way out of his predicament.

"This trick is yours, Kinnard, but there'll be

another time. I'll square my account against you."

Kinnard nodded, a faint amusement in the depths of his gray eyes. It was such talk as he had heard before.

"Whenever you're ready," he said quietly.

Turning his back on Arnett, he walked away. It presented the latter with an opportunity that he was briefly tempted to exploit. A flash of sense stopped him. Going to his horse, he swung up and quickly put the Crossing behind him.

4

The Buckmaster crew was in the yard, washed up and waiting for supper, three evenings later, when they saw a rider coming up the creek. It sent Ike Jarvis to the door.

"Company comin', Jesse," he called inside to Buckmaster. Jamie stepped out with her father.

"It's Mr. Kinnard, Dad!" she said with a little rush of excitement.

But if she was pleased one moment, she was distressed the next as she recalled his promise to see her before he left. She had no reason to believe other than that he had come to say goodby.

"There's no noise about this man, Jamie," Jesse Buckmaster observed approvingly as Kinnard started across the yard. "I'll never forget how he faded Worth the other day and made him crawl. I didn't believe anybody could do that to Worth."

"I hope you won't mention it," said Jamie. "Any trouble he's had with him is his affair, not ours."

Jesse wasn't as sure of that as she was. He said nothing, but he gave her a searching, sidelong glance and asked himself if she was as unaware as she made out that the enmity between Arnett and this man from the north could be over her.

Kinnard received a friendly greeting from the

Buckmasters and the crew. Young Lin Runnels offered to put up his horse.

"That won't be necessary," said Kinnard. "I won't be staying long. I'll leave him here at the rack."

"You'll stay for supper," Jamie informed him.

Kinnard grinned.

"I'm as bad as a grubline rider; I seem always to show up at mealtime."

He could see that things were at a standstill. There was no evidence that anything had been done about preparing to move. Jesse Buckmaster appeared to be throwing off his despondency, but it was apparent that he didn't have the heart to begin tearing down the comfort and security he had wrought for Jamie and himself, here on Ten Mile Creek. Jamie came close to reading the thought running through Kinnard's mind.

"We'll be able to take so little with us when we go," she said. "It means leaving so much behind that we don't know where to begin."

"I understand," he told her. "I been doing some riding the past couple days. It's the same wherever I've gone. Folks are stunned; they don't know what to do. . . . Are you still of a mind to try for Montana?"

"We're set on that," Jesse informed him with a touch of his old spirit. "I don't know that we'll ever git there. We'll be all right up into Kansas, as far as the Santa Fe. Maybe I can hire a trail boss in one of them railway towns to take us the rest of the way."

"I can get you there, Jesse, if—"

Jamie couldn't believe her ears.

"But you told me you weren't interested in hiring out for wages," she cried, a puzzled look on her young face.

"I'm not, mam. I've bought some cattle—eleven hundred head, to be exact—all young stuff. No calves, but young stuff that will do fifteen miles a day. I would have liked to buy more, but that was as far as my money would take me. I thought if you were agreeable we might throw your herd and mine together. We'd have to hire another man or two. I'd expect you to pay their wages—you couldn't get along without a couple more men even if you went by yourself. You won't owe me anything. As for the grub, I'll pay for my share."

It was so unexpected that the Buckmasters were incredulous at first. The glance they exchanged swiftly changed from bewilderment to pleased surprise.

"It'll give us a chance, Dad—a real chance!" Jamie cried, her voice trembling with eagerness. "Do you realize how fortunate we are to have such an opportunity offered us?"

"It suits me fine," Jesse declared, a grin on his bearded face for the first time in days. "I'll take you up, Kinnard. I don't know how well acquainted you are with the country to the north, but I've seen enough of you to be convinced that you're a man who knows what he's doin'. Every outfit that's movin' will be takin' on extra men for the trail. Good men may be hard to find. I reckon I can locate a couple. Whose stuff did you buy?"

"I got most of them from Deb Karnes and a couple hundred from Jeff Sarles. I'd like to pick them up tomorrow and move them over here."

"We can do it. It ain't far. You stay here tonight and me and the boys will go with you in the mornin'. Karnes had two good men workin' for him. We can speak to 'em."

"No use doing that," said Kinnard. "They've caught on with the 44 outfit already. Nick Brewster isn't losing any time. We'd do well to follow his example. We ought to be moving in three or four days."

"Wal, we can do it," Jesse agreed reluctantly.

It gave him a wrench to be pinned down, but he had someone to tell him what to do now. Jamie realized that it was what he needed.

Honey called them in to supper. Over the table they discussed their plans. The crew felt at liberty to join in the conversation, especially old Ike Jarvis. Young Lin Runnels, Johnny Gaines and he were impressed with Kinnard. Knowing they were to have him with them went a long way toward freeing them from their doubts and misgivings. They sensed that long before they saw the Missouri Bad Lands it would be his orders, rather than Jesse's, that they would be taking.

"We'll be headin' for Dodge, I reckon," Ike suggested.

"No, we'll give it a wide berth, Ike. With the amount of cattle going north the cow thieves around Dodge City will be in clover. You'll hear of whole herds being stolen. We'll stay well to the east and slip across the Sante Fe tracks and go up west of Ellsworth. We'll be needing supplies by that time. We can go in for them. We'll hit out for Ogalalla, Nebraska, then and cross the North Platte at Camp Clark. Ogalalla will be the jumping off place for us; it'll be our last chance to stock up."

"What about grass, Mr. Kinnard?" asked Jamie. "Will we have trouble finding it?"

"In places. We'll have more trouble finding water. And there'll be other troubles—man-made, I mean. If I may ask, mam, where are you going to locate till your father is settled in Montana?"

The question startled Jamie.

"Why, I'm going with you. I thought that was understood."

Kinnard was dumbfounded. His annoyance flowed across his face and he did not attempt to dissemble it.

"That would be impossible, mam." He kept

his voice down, but it was charged with feeling. "You haven't any idea what you'd be letting yourself in for. We'll be driving north for ten to twelve weeks. There'll be no comforts. It means sleeping on the ground, fighting the weather, fording streams and doing fifteen miles a day, no matter what we run into. It'll be hard enough on the men. Believe me, mam, you just couldn't stand up to it, day after day."

"You're saying that because I'm a woman," Jamie retorted with indignation. "I've slept on the ground and lived in a wagon for years. And I did a man's work, too."

"She's right, Kinnard," said Jesse. "In the years when we was driftin' back and forth across the Panhandle, a covered wagon was her only home. As for her ridin', I'll put her up against any man at this table."

"They don't come any better, Kinnard," Ike Jarvis declared stoutly. "The girl's as tough as an old mossy horn steer. And she's got a lot of cow savvy. I guarantee you she won't hold us up."

They argued the matter all through supper. Against his better judgment, Kinnard gave ground. He gazed across the table at Jamie. She met his eyes with head unbowed.

"Do you realize, mam, that when we pull out my job will be more than just to find grass and water and get us through? I'll have to hold myself responsible for the safety of the herd and the whole outfit. There will be differences of opinion at times. When we can't come to agree, it'll have to be my judgment that prevails. Do you agree to that?"

"Naturally. Someone's got to have the final word."

"And you, Jesse?" Kinnard inquired.

Jesse Buckmaster pulled at his beard for a moment or two and nodded soberly.

"If you hold a man responsible for gittin' you through, then you got to rely on his judgment. No question about that."

"If that's understood, then I'm agreeable to Jamie going with us far as Ellsworth. When we get there, it'll be up to me to decide whether she goes on or not. Is that fair enough?"

"It's fine with me," Jamie beamed. "If I can't prove myself by the time we get that far, then I don't deserve to go on."

In these days of disaster every man was watching the other, suspicious of what he was doing, or was about to do. It followed that word got around quickly. A few hours after Kinnard bought the bulk of Deb Karnes' small herd and a couple hundred yearling steers from Jeff Sarles the news reached Arnett. It so aroused his curiosity that he put aside his own concern and followed it up. It did not take him long to learn that the stock had been thrown in with Jesse Buckmaster's herd, and what their plans were.

By a characteristic bit of skullduggery he had secured an old Army scout, familiar with the country to the north, to pilot his outfit. It had been his intention to sell Jesse the idea that they should combine their outfits. It was too late for that now. His cup of bitterness overflowed when he heard that Jamie was going with the drive. Thought of Kinnard and her being together for weeks and imperiling his chances of getting his hands on the Buckmaster herd filled him with black, jealous rage. Though he knew he had little chance of talking Jesse out of the arrangement he had made, he was determined to try. Instead of going directly to the ranch, he went to the Crossing first, in the hope that he might run into him there.

Of the handful of people who lived at Canadian Crossing, some were gone already. Jep Wright was packing up. He was going back to Texas. There was little left on his shelves.

"Jesse was in yesterday," Jep informed him. "Lookin' to take on some extra men. He picked up a good one in Jim Travis. I don't know about the other one. Of course it ain't every man who will go north."

"Who is he, Jep?"

"Steve Portugay. He's a reckless fool. Never sticks at anythin'."

Arnett's interest quickened at once. He was better acquainted with Steve Portugay than he had ever given anyone reason to suspect. On his rise to his present affluence, he had always found Portugay a willing and reliable tool for handling matters that wouldn't stand the light of day.

"What about the string of broncs Steve was breaking?"

"He's agreed to git rid of 'em in a day or two."

That told Arnett what he wanted to know. When he left the Crossing, he went straight up the river to Portugay's shack. He didn't waste any time getting to the point.

"I hear you're going north with Jesse Buckmaster and this new man Kinnard. What's the idea, Steve?"

It drew an uncertain shrug from Portugay.

"He offered me good money. I got a sorta hankerin' to go north for once. I guess that's it."

He showed his white, even teeth in a faintly amused grin.

He was a rather short, wiry man, with a swarthy skin and crinkly hair that was as black as midnight. Arnett had never asked but he suspected that the blood of several races flowed in Portugay's veins. Though he smiled a great deal, there was something cruel and merciless in his face. His movements were quick and definite, like the striking of a rattler.

"You got somethin' on your mind," he speculated, his eyes blank and inscrutable. "You don't want me to go with Buckmaster and Kinnard?"

"That's perfect. That's why I'm here, Steve. I want you to do a job for me." He pulled out his wallet and counted off ten ten-dollar bills and thrust them into the other's hand. "That's a little on account. There'll be more as we go along."

"You always pay well." Portugay's white teeth flashed in another grin. "No use me playing dumb with you. I been hearin' how Kinnard's been beatin' your time. That's the job you want done, ain't it—on him I mean—"

"Yes, by God, it is! I want you to make him look bad, Steve. There's hundred ways you can foul him up—something today, something else tomorrow. I want the Buckmasters to get so damned sick of him before they reach Ellsworth that they'll split with him when they get there."

Little Steve stared at him until he was satisfied that he had read the other's mind. With a knowing smirk, he said:

"That'd leave old Jess damn near helpless. If you should happen to show up jest about then, he'd leap at the chance to throw in with you."

"And so?"

"It ain't hard to figger," the little man returned with a careless shrug. "I'd expect you to swallow him up like you did old man Whitmire and a couple others I could mention."

Arnett wanted to slap him down for his

insolence. But he knew he couldn't afford to quarrel with Portugay.

"You got a loose tongue, Steve," he said thinly. "If you're going to be worth anything to me, you'll tie a knot in it. Your outfit will be pulling out four or five days before I can get moving. But we'll catch up and keep a few miles behind you. If you want to find me, you'll know where to look. . . . Do we understand each other?"

"Yeh—as far as it goes. Let's put the rest of it on the line. If the chance comes, do you want me to gun him?"

He was as matter-of-fact about it as though they were discussing last year's election. A contemptuous smirk touched the corners of his mouth as Arnett took an unduly long time over his answer. It was by such little things that his respect for a man went up or down.

The truth was that Arnett was not ready for such drastic action, however desirable it might be.

"We'll see how things go for a couple weeks," he said woodenly. "But it's something to keep in mind, Steve."

5

They had been moving for five days and not doing too well. Kinnard had not complained at first; he knew it always took two or three days for a trail herd to settle down to steady going. It was time for improvement, but it did not come; according to his calculations they were not making better than ten miles a day, though this Oklahoma country was the easiest going they were likely to find on the long journey north. Water and grass were no problem.

It had become routine with him to range far ahead every morning as soon as the herd had been put in motion. He was usually back by late noon, with a suitable spot located for a bed-ground for that night. It gave him an opportunity to observe how the crew were doing their job. He had perforce to regard Jamie and her father as working members of the crew. He had them riding point. It was an important job, but for the present it didn't call for the hard work that fell to the lot of the two swing men and the two who were on the flank.

He had had no fault to find with Jamie or with anyone else, for that matter. But he sensed that something was wrong. He couldn't believe it was entirely due to the fact that they were short-handed for the size of the herd they were driving. Ike Jarvis, Lin Runnels and little Johnny Gaines, the old Buckmaster crew, did their work well. So did Jim Travis, the new man. He didn't know about Steve Portugay. The other men were not unacquainted with Steve. They showed no sign of warming up to him, but they got along together. That was good enough for Kinnard.

It was later than usual this afternoon when he returned to the herd and found it strung out for several miles. Believing there was no excuse for it, he circled wide to get out of the dust and rode back to the stragglers at once. His temper was short when he got there. Portugay was riding drag and apparently unable to push the stuff ahead any faster.

"How did you happen to let them get strung out like this?" Kinnard demanded sharply. "We won't do better than eight miles today."

"I been doin' my best," was the unruffled answer. Portugay was carrying out Arnett's instructions, and that precluded him from resenting any criticism. "You said yourself that this is a two-man job back here."

"I know," Kinnard conceded, "but that's no excuse for letting the stuff get strung out. I'll stay back here and give you a hand till we bed down for the night."

Between them they got the stragglers moving a bit faster and the herd closed up some. It didn't satisfy Kinnard. Darting here and there, never still for a minute, shouting and slapping his coiled rope at the recalcitrant cows, he drove them on. Through the clouds of dust he could see Portugay working as hard as he.

They met briefly as evening came on.

"You see how it goes," the little man observed smugly. "It's always this way with a mixed herd. That young stuff of yours is walkin' the legs off Buckmaster's old cows. They keep workin' back to the rear. That slows the whole herd up."

This was so well known to anyone who had ever handled a trail herd that Kinnard resented having it presented to him as something that was beyond his knowledge. But Steve was not taking him for a fool of that sort. To the contrary, he surmised that the other knew as well as he did that, sooner or later, the old cows would have to be sacrificed, and that Kinnard, knowing Buckmaster would bitterly oppose such a suggestion, had refrained from mentioning it. Portugay's hidden purpose was to force the issue.

"I don't suppose Jesse would ever agree to it," he continued, "but we won't ever make any time till forty to fifty of these old flea bags are shot or turned adrift. Why don't you tell him so, Kinnard?"

Though he missed its real significance, it rubbed the latter the wrong way, and with hot resentment, he said:

"I'll play my own cards, Portugay. There may be times when I'll want advice. If so, I'll ask for it."

The little man shrugged off the rebuke and let it go at that. Riding drag, he had seen something that he was sure would bring matters to a head between Kinnard and the Buckmasters in a day or two. He felt he was in the position of a man with a double-barreled shotgun; if one barrel didn't go off, the other would.

Darkness had fallen by the time the stock had been watered and bedded down that evening. It made supper so late that even Honey Williams, the cook, usually bubbling over with chuckling good humor, was grumpy and out of sort. As soon as he had eaten, Johnny Gaines went out to stand the first watch over the horses and the herd for the night. The others sat around the fire for half an hour. There was little companionship in the fire this evening; only Steve Portugay seemed unperturbed by the disappointing eight to nine miles they had progressed that day. The wind was rising and there was a suspicious dampness in the air.

"We're goin' to git a wettin' before mornin'," Ike Jarvis prophesied. "Some lightnin' off there to the west right now."

It didn't matter. They expected to get a good many wettings before they saw Montana.

The magnitude of the undertaking in which

they were engaged had begun to oppress Jesse Buckmaster. Jamie watched him across the fire, a huddled, somehow lonely figure, his dead pipe clamped between his teeth. Hoping to cheer him, she said:

"It was just a bad day, Dad. We'll do better tomorrow."

"And for a good many tomorrows if we're ever goin' to git there," Jesse responded without removing his pipe from his mouth. Putting it away, he shook his head soberly. "I don't know what's wrong. We ain't got nobody ahead of us holdin' us back."

Consciously or otherwise, it seemed to imply a criticism of the way the drive was being handled.

Kinnard caught Portugay regarding him with a taunting light in his black eyes. He sensed that the little man was daring him to speak out. But he was not to be baited or hurried into taking a stand with the Buckmasters, in regard to the old cows. Another two or three days couldn't matter much. By then the action that he knew must be taken would be so clearly indicated that they would have to agree to it. But if this moment accomplished nothing else, it confirmed his feeling that Steve Portugay was a man to be watched.

Jamie turned to Kinnard. She no longer addressed him as Mr. Kinnard; they had become too well acquainted for that.

"Frank, I know you're as anxious as we are

to do better than nine to ten miles a day. I know it isn't your fault that we're not, but isn't there something that can be done?"

"I'm going to switch things around a bit tomorrow. That may help."

As he had got to know her better, his admiration had deepened. The fondness he had come to have for her had no romantic undertones, or so he chose to believe. There were moments, however, when he wondered if he was deceiving himself, if it wasn't really the woman in her that appealed so strongly to him rather than the impersonal, undemanding, almost man-to-man regard that had sprung up between them and which he found pleasant indeed. She was free of the wiles and feminine guile he had come to detest in women. There was an honest forthrightness about her that he had never found in others. She was a lady—but she was no angel, either. She had a temper and a will of her own. When a steer busted out of the herd one afternoon and gave her an argument about being turned back, she resorted to some very unlady-like language in her exasperation. When she had hazed the animal back into the herd, she glanced across at him and caught his grinning. "Sorry you heard," she called out, without being sorry at all. "Some of these critters just don't seem to understand sweet talk." A man remembered little things like that.

"I'm going to have you ride point alone during

the morning, Jamie," he continued. "I'll drop two men back to ride drag. Steve's been back there for three or four days. It's a tough job." He glanced at Portugay. "You'll ride flank tomorrow with Johnny. Ike and Travis will take your place. Jesse, you and Lin will ride swing. We'll see how that works. I'll get back as early as I can and side you the rest of the day, Jamie. Can you handle the job alone?"

"I think so—"

"If you have any trouble, Steve can move up with you."

He was putting the little man where he could be watched. He did it so adroitly that Portugay had no reason to take offense. For a few minutes they talked over the new alignment.

"I don't have to tell you what to do, Ike," Kinnard said to the old man. "Just don't let the stuff get strung out the way it was yesterday."

Portugay walked over to the wagon, a satisfied smile on his swarthy face. He thought he knew what was likely to happen when Ike and Travis began throwing the prod into the old cows. Getting an ax, he chopped down some willow limbs and stacked them up against the windward side of the wagon.

"That was thoughtful of you, Steve," said Jamie when he came back to the fire. She slept beneath the wagon.

Rain drops were spattering them already.

"I don't know how much of a storm this is goin' to be," he told her. "The branches may keep you from gittin' a bad wettin'."

Crazy ideas were running through his head. This wasn't the first time he had played up to her. Kinnard had not noticed before. It set him to wondering tonight.

The wind was scattering the fire.

"Time to turn in," Jesse announced, stamping it out.

When Kinnard returned to the herd at noon and fell in beside Jamie, he could see that she had had a hard morning. She was as cheerful as ever but she looked tired.

"We're doing better up to now than yesterday," he told her. "You must have been hazing the stuff right along."

"We saved some time getting started, Frank. The stock was on good grass last evening. Dad didn't think it was necessary to let them have two hours' grazing this morning. We got moving a few minutes after Honey pulled out with the wagon."

He nodded approvingly.

"Good idea, Jamie. Let's not lose what we've gained. We'll eat dinner in shifts today; I'll send half the crew in at a time and keep the herd moving right along."

He was at the wagon when Ike Jarvis came in to eat. He got him aside.

"How are things going back there, Ike?"

"Not good, and they're goin' to git worse. I reckon you know what the trouble is as well as I do."

"The old cows?"

"Yeh. I knew some of 'em hadn't calved yet. They're about ready to drop 'em now. I miss my guess if we don't have some little strangers in camp, come mornin'."

It was no more than Portugay could have told him the previous evening. Kinnard wasn't surprised; he had foreseen that one thing or another would make a showdown with Jesse Buckmaster unavoidable.

"You know what will have to be done, Ike."

"Sure. Jesse won't like it. You'll jest have to take the bit in your teeth."

As the afternoon wore on the herd began to string out again. The cattle had been without water all day. By five o'clock, the bed-ground for the night was not far ahead. A small creek was handy. They smelled it and began to move faster. But again the stragglers were late getting in. In the morning, just after daybreak, it was Steve Portugay who came in to breakfast with the news that four or five of the old cows had dropped calves during the night. Jamie and her father went out to see them at once.

Kinnard was waiting for them when they got back. Jamie was flushed with excitement.

"They're the prettiest things you ever saw, Frank." His dour countenance put an effective wet blanket on her enthusiasm. She checked herself and said: "What's the matter?"

"This is an unfortunate business. You should understand that, Jamie."

"What do you mean?"

"I mean what are we going to do with them? We can't take them with us."

"Are you suggesting that we leave them behind?" she demanded indignantly. "The wolves would pull them down soon as we got out of sight."

"I daresay they would," he conceded. "But there's no one we can give them to. We've got to face it; the only thing to do is to have them destroyed."

"Now wait a minute," Jesse burst out. "They're my calves, Kinnard. It's purty high-handed of you to say what's to be done with them. That's up to me."

"Well, suggest something," Kinnard invited. He knew this was a prelude to the real showdown that must come between Buckmaster and himself, and he was determined not to lose his temper over it. "Do you want us to sit here for two or three weeks until those calves are strong enough to walk a few miles? You're an experienced stockman. You know how far they'd get if we waited a month or two. You and Jamie talk it over for a few minutes and let me know what you want to do."

Turning on his heel, he walked away. The horses had been brought in. He was saddling his roan gelding when Jesse came up.

"Reckon there's nothin' to do but let you have your way about it," he grumbled tartly.

"It's not so much my way but the only way to handle it," Kinnard said pointedly.

He told Johnny Gaines and Portugay to round up the calves and take them down the creek and shoot them.

"The rest of you be ready to turn back their mammies if they try to follow."

It gave them a late start. It resulted in still another poor day. They were a glum lot as they sat around the fire that evening. Steve Portugay seemed to be the only one left with a laugh in him. Jamie had not exchanged a word with Kinnard throughout the afternoon, and what little she had to say this evening was not directed at him. When she got up to go to the wagon to get a leather jacket, he followed her.

"I don't want to inflict myself on you, Jamie," he said, "but isn't it a little bit silly for you to go on being angry with me over what happened this morning? You've had time enough to think it over and cool down."

"It isn't the calves," she informed him icily. "I know you were right, but you didn't have to take the decision out of Dad's hands. I hate arrogance in a man. I didn't like it in Worth Arnett and I don't like it in you."

"I didn't know I was being arrogant," he protested. "I've got a job to do; it's up to me to get this outfit through. Of course, if you don't like the way I'm handling things, that's something else."

"I have no fault to find on the score, Frank. You know that. You're doing your utmost—"

"But it ain't good enough. I expected to reach the Kansas line in two weeks. Right now it looks like we'll be lucky to make it in three. I have a little property in Deadwood. It doesn't amount to much. Aside from that, every dollar I own is tied up in my part of this herd. I've got to get through in good time for my own sake, as much as for yours."

She had nothing to say for the moment.

"There something wrong, Jamie," he went on. "I know what it is. It's no secret; you and your father are the only ones who refuse to see it."

"Well!" she exclaimed aghast. "I don't know whether to be angry or frightened. If you know what's wrong, why haven't you said somethin'?"

"I'm reluctant to say anything—knowing how it will be received. The argument over the calves this morning wouldn't be a patch to it."

"Frank, I've got to know," she said, her voice off key in its urgency. "What is it?"

"It's the old cows. We got upwards of fifty head that should never have been put on the trail. They do all right for a few hours early in the day. They begin working back through the herd in the afternoon and wind up every day in the drag. They're getting slower, day by day. There's only one thing to do, Jamie—weed them out and destroy them."

"Oh, no!" she cried, horrified at the thought. "Dad would never consent to that. If you only knew how he's slaved and scrimped to put our little herd together, you wouldn't even suggest it. Please, Frank, don't mention it to him. He understands that some of the old stock will drop before we see Montana. If a cow goes down and has to be shot, that's one thing; but to kill them wholesale—forty to fifty head—is asking too much. Please don't say anything, Frank . . . please!"

"Maybe it won't be necessary for me to say anything. I'm going to ask him to ride drag for a couple days. It'll give him a chance to see for himself that it's the old stuff that's holding us back."

They crossed the Salt Fork of the Arkansas two days later. Putting the herd across the river cost time. But though the afternoon was well along, they went on for three miles and bedded down on a grassy flat beside a shallow, meandering creek. They were still not averaging better than ten miles a day. If riding drag had opened Jesse Buckmaster's eyes to the unescapable, he kept it to himself. But it was easy to see from his morose, brooding manner that something was weighing on him. Kinnard wasn't in any doubt as to what it was.

Ike Jarvis was the last man in that evening. He went to the creek at once and washed up. As he sat down to eat, he said:

"We got another outfit right behind us. They're acrost the Salt Fork and beddin' down on the north bank."

"Big outfit, Ike?" Kinnard asked.

"Sizeable."

"I ain't surprised." Kinnard's tone expressed his displeasure. "We got away first, but we been just slogging along, letting the advantage slip away from us. We'll pay for it later on."

Jamie knew what he was saying was for her father's ears, but all Jesse had to say was, "We're doin' our best."

If Kinnard was not surprised to have another outfit on their heels, neither was Steve Portugay. He fancied he knew who was moving up on them. The trail they were leaving, with its night-camps was as easy to follow as a string of beads.

He was first man out on night-guard this evening. He had been out only thirty to forty minutes when he came pounding back with word that two of their horses had broken away and were heading back toward the Salt Fork.

"If you'll send a man out to take my place, I'll go after those broncs, Frank."

"Go ahead," Kinnard told him.

Portugay had driven the two horses into a little valley where the grass was good. He knew he would find them there when he wanted them. Once out of sight of the camp, he swung south to the river. In less than half an hour he was talking to Arnett. The tall Texan enjoyed what the little man had to tell him.

"I knew you folks were having trouble, Steve, the way you been poking along," he said with unholy satisfaction. "I been behind you for two or three days. Been a job to hold back so I wouldn't run over you."

"I tied some knots in Kinnard's tail," Portugay observed with a shameless grin. "It's a crazy outfit, Worth. Kinnard knows his business, but the old man and the girl have got him hamstrung. The lid damn near blew off when he had the calves killed. She wouldn't speak to him for a day. Jesse goes around with his mouth pulled down in his whiskers. It's buildin' up to somethin', I tell you. That old stuff will have to be shot. Kinnard may hold off for three or four days, but when he gives the word, the fur will fly."

"Good! That's what I want to hear. Can't you hurry it up, Steve?"

"I don't know as I can. But I can give it a twist that'll add to the hard feelin's." He rolled a contemplative cigarette. "While we're waitin' for that matter to boil up, you could make a little trouble for Kinnard?"

"Yeh, how's that?"

"He sends only one man out at a time to night-guard the stock—cows and broncs. Three or four hosses are kept on pins near the wagon, the rest are sent out. It would be a cinch to run 'em off. You could drive 'em a few miles and let 'em go—make it look a hoss thief job that went wrong. I'll be on the midnight shift tomorrow night." His black eyes were bright, with cunning. "Get me?"

"Yeh—"

"Shouldn't be any trick to make Buckmaster see it was Kinnard's fault, night-guardin' with only one man."

"I'm damned if you ain't good, Steve!" Arnett chuckled with hearty approval. "I'll put on a show for Kinnard and make it look like the real thing."

After they had talked it over for a few minutes, Portugay didn't linger long. With a boldness and nonchalance that were flattering to his ego, he recovered the horses that allegedly had decamped and drove them back into the *caballada* and resumed his night-guarding.

Kinnard threw a questioning glance at Johnny

Gaines when the latter came up to the fire, a few minutes later.

"He just got back," said Johnny. "He had the broncs with him. He had quite a ride."

"I imagine he did." The words came from Kinnard's lips with an ugly inference. He got up to seek his blankets. "Maybe a ride was what he wanted," he added in the same tone.

"How's that?" Johnny said, sorely puzzled.

"You're the last one up," said Kinnard, ignoring the question. "When you get through with the fire, put it out. It's going to blow a bit tonight."

6

In the gray dawn, when Jamie sat up in her blankets, she found that Kinnard had finished breakfast and had his horse saddled. Rubbing the sleep out of her eyes, she said:

"You are getting an early start. Any particular reason?"

"No, I just thought I'd be able to get back sooner and make your job a bit easier. I was over this country just ahead yesterday. You won't have any trouble pointing the stuff. You'll see a line of low hills when you get out a mile or two. Just keep to the west of them."

She called him back as he started away.

"Frank, this outfit that's come up behind us—I'm worried."

"There's no reason to be," he said reassuringly. "We'll have one bunch or another behind us a good part of the time from now on—and ahead of us, too. As long as water is as easy to find as it has been, we shouldn't have any trouble. I expect this particular outfit will drive past us during the morning. That's another reason I want to get an early start; I want to be sure we have water tonight."

He looked long and far for it. Early in the morning he located a small, weedy pond that, judging by its wide, muddy shoreline, was rapidly drying up as the days grew longer and warmer. A pair of mud hens had it to themselves. It was not what he was looking for. But as he went on, the country changed noticeably; the grass thinned and the wide sweep of the prairie was dotted with dwarf sage. He tried the west first, and finding no sign of springs or running water, he struck off for the hills to the east that he had mentioned to Jamie. They marched along for miles. But they, too, had changed into barren mounds of sand.

The shrunken pond that he had disdained began to take on importance. He judged he was eighteen miles from the herd when he turned back. Noon had come and gone when Jamie saw him returning. His tardy appearance prepared her for what he had to say.

"We'll use the pond and be glad we've got it," she declared. "The water is warm, I suppose."

"The stock will drink it. That's all that's necessary. I'd heard about these Oklahoma sand hills. We could have gone up to the east of them, but this was a short-cut." He was visibly displeased with himself. "Like most short-cuts, it isn't going to pan out. We won't do more than a miserable few miles today and face tough going tomorrow."

She refused to be discouraged.

"How far are we from the pond?"

"Between three and four miles." He changed

the subject abruptly. "When your father came in this noon, did he have anything to say about the outfit that's in back of us?"

"He thinks they're either getting a mighty late start, or don't intend to move today. Up to noon, he and Ike saw no sign of a moving dust cloud on our back trail."

"There's dust over there to the west of us right now. It's moving right along, too."

Jamie finally located it, upwards of two miles away. She took it for granted that the dust was being kicked up by a trail herd, and very likely the one that had been behind them the previous evening.

Responding to a sudden decision, Kinnard said:

"I'm going to ride over that way. If I get within half a mile of them, I'll be able to determine what their intentions are for tonight."

She caught her breath, thinking she understood what he was saying.

"You mean they may be heading for the pond, Frank?"

"Very likely, if they got a man with them who is acquainted with this country north of the Salt Fork and knows water is going to be hard to find for a day or two. It would explain their late start."

"How's that?"

"Why, figuring I'm a stranger to this country, they'd give me a chance to pass up the pond and look for better water further north. That would give them the pond without any argument and give us a dry camp tonight."

Jamie gave him a shrewd, searching glance.

"You seem to take it for granted that they know who we are."

"I don't think there's any question about that," he answered shortly. "I won't be gone long."

Her eyes followed him as he rode away. More than ever before, she realized how much she had come to depend on him. He wasn't always easy to get along with. There was a reserved, unbending aloofness about him that was forbidding at times. About himself, he had nothing to say, and though she had known him now for several weeks, and rather intimately, she knew him but little better than the first evening he had stopped at the ranch on Ten Mile Creek. But whatever his background—and she often wondered about it—he had the instincts and manners of a gentleman.

"I don't know what we'd do without him," she mused.

When he was still some distance away the wind carried to Kinnard's ears the protesting bellowing of cattle that were being driven along faster than they wanted to go. By taking advantage of an intervening ridge, he gained a position well in advance of the oncoming herd and close enough to satisfy him. Without showing himself, he waited for the drive to come up. An old-timer, shriveled and bewhiskered, was leading it. At his side rode Worth Arnett, so tall in the saddle that there was no mistaking him.

Kinnard was not in the least surprised.

"I had the right hunch," he muttered.

That hunch sprang from his suspicion that Steve Portugay's story about the two horses that had broken away, and the long time it had taken to recover them, was a tale the little man had invented to permit him to visit the camp on the bank of the Salt Fork. That Portugay had found it necessary to resort to such trickery to visit the camp could be explained only because he had reason to believe that it was the camp of one who was not on friendly terms with Kinnard. To the latter, that had narrowed it down to Arnett at once. But it neither told him who it was that Steve was so anxious to see, nor why.

"I don't like the trickery of it," he speculated as he waited, "but otherwise it could have been innocent enough; he may have a pal riding with Arnett, or someone who owes him a little money."

It occurred to him with something of a start that that might include Arnett himself.

"No matter," he decided. "I can't do anything about it now. I'll keep it in mind."

He counted twelve men in Arnett's outfit, included Arnett, the old-timer who was his trail boss, his cook and swamper, who drove the two wagons. The wagons jolted past Kinnard. They were well ahead of the herd, but some distance behind Arnett and the old man. The latter stood up in his stirrups now and getting the attention of the drivers, motioned for them to cut back to the east. That was the direction in which the pond lay. Kinnard didn't waste any more time. He came swinging back to his own outfit at a driving gallop.

"It's Arnett," he rapped out brusquely. "They're heading for the pond. We can beat them to it if we get a move on. You drop back and tell Johnny and Steve we're going to run the young stuff; I'll tell Lin and Jim Travis."

"What about the rest of the herd?"

"Bring it along as best you can. You don't have to hurry. I'll hold that water if I can get there first with a few hundred head."

"Frank, this is shaping up to a fight," she said quickly.

"Good trail law says if you find water it's yours. We'll stand on that." He was suddenly gruff with her. "Swing your horse around and tell Johnny and Steve what we're doing."

Lopping off the head of the herd from the rest of the column took time. Once it was accomplished, the yearlings and two-year-olds began to widen the gap. Presently Kinnard and his men had them moving so fast that Honey Williams had to whip up his four-horse team to keep ahead of them.

They were no more than a mile from the pond

when Arnett's outfit poured over a rise in the undulating prairie and came on relentlessly. The pace at which it was moving told Kinnard that Arnett had been apprised of his maneuver and was racing for the water now.

"We got 'em faded, Frank!" Lin Runnels yelled triumphantly.

Steve Portugay was silent, but the others took up the cry. Kinnard did not respond. He could see that the pond was theirs. Holding onto it might be something else.

When they reached it, the cows plunged into the water up to their knees. The soft mud bottom became churned up in a few minutes as they floundered about. Honey unhitched his team and led it around to the far side where the water was not yet riled.

Kinnard called Portugay and the others around him. Arnett's outfit was by now no more than a third of a mile away and coming on without any sign of deviating an inch.

"We're in possession," said Kinnard, "and I'm not going to give up this mudhole. Arnett's got us badly outnumbered. If any of you don't like the odds and want to pull out, this is the time to say so."

The others declared their loyalty to him, as he was sure they would. It put Portugay on the spot. The little man didn't hesitate. He knew he couldn't afford to.

"You needn't worry about me," he growled. "I'll go all the way with you." He couldn't see any other course to take.

Kinnard surmised as much.

"Thank you, Steve," he grunted. "Just don't get itchy-fingered and reach for your gun."

A wicked, fleeting twitch disturbed Portugay's thin lips. He couldn't decide whether it was just advice or a warning that Kinnard had delivered. It was both.

Arnett and his bearded trail boss spurred ahead now and did not pull up until they were within speaking distance.

"I got a lot of thirsty cattle, Kinnard," the tall man whipped out belligerently. "I'm going to share this water."

"You try it and I'll change your mind for you," Kinnard informed him, his words packed with a cool, deliberate insolence.

Arnett did not appear to be impressed.

"You're getting a little big for your britches, ain't you?" he inquired. "I got men enough to have my way about this."

"If you think so, try it," was Kinnard's flinty response. "Your little game of holding back this morning so we'd pass up this water didn't work. If you want to be well advised, Arnett, you'll swing off to the west before it's too late." To his men, he said, "Two hundred yards is the deadline; if that stuff crosses it, use your guns."

It was melodramatic, even theatrical, but there was a deadly earnestness about it that carried conviction. If Worth Arnett wanted a showdown, here it was, with the odds in his favor. His handsome face was livid with hatred as he glared at Kinnard. He knew he had a crew that, to a man, would do his bidding. There was no doubt in his mind as to who would win if he let this matter go to a decision. The desire to embrace this opportunity was so strong in him that he trembled under its impact. But there was Jamie Buckmaster to be considered; his fight was with Kinnard, not with her. She was the pearl beyond price with him. In spite of his hatred and insane jealousy, he saw clearly enough that his problem was to rid himself of one without losing the other. It gave him pause; there were circumstances connected with this moment that would not advance his cause with Jamie if he proceeded with it.

He motioned the old man up beside him and they conversed briefly. Kinnard couldn't catch what they were saying, but the old man was evidently insisting on something and pointing off to the northwest.

"Anyone know the old character?" Kinnard inquired.

"That's Cimmaron Smith," Jim Travis told him. "Old Cim's an ex-Army scout. He knows this country as good as anybody."

"Doubtless he does, Jim, but if he's telling Arnett there's water in another pond off there to the northwest, he's wrong. There's a pond, all right—'bout the size of this one—but it's dry."

Arnett reached a decision. Without giving Kinnard and his crew a glance, he rode off with Cimmaron Smith and the signal was given for the point men to swing the herd to the northwest.

"By God, you bluffed him out, Frank!" Johnny Gaines declared with relief and no little amazement. "We coulda held 'em off a few minutes. But there was too many of 'em; they'd have made mincemeat of us."

"Arnett was all set for trouble," said Lin. "What do you suppose it was that made him change his mind?"

Kinnard shook his head.

"I don't believe he changed his mind about anything. He was doing the bluffing, not me. You can be sure of one thing: this ain't the end of it. Arnett will make us some more trouble." He flicked a quick glance at Portugay. "Ain't that right, Steve?"

It took the little man by surprise.

"How the hell should I know?" he jerked out. His anger was with himself for having been caught off guard. "If he didn't pull away from the Salt Fork till noon, he's sure got a fast-movin' outfit," he went on, trying to cover up. "Chances are we won't see no more of him."

Kinnard let it go at that. He was satisfied that he had given Portugay a jolt. Leaving Lin and Johnny at the pond, he went back with the others to help bring the rest of the herd in. Jesse had come up to give Jamie a hand; Ike Jarvis was back in the drag alone. She and her father were entitled to an explanation.

"No," he said in answer to Jamie's question, "we didn't have any real trouble. We had an argument, but that's all. The water was ours and I refused to be pushed off. Arnett's idea was that he was going to share it with us."

"Was that so unreasonable, Frank? If there was water enough—"

"No, you can't mix trail herds!" Jesse said, flatly. "We'd been all day separatin' 'em. Worth wouldn't let another outfit move in on him. We don't want no trouble with him nor anyone else, but we ain't goin' to be pushed around. You did right, Kinnard."

It was the first time in days that Buckmaster had voiced such wholehearted approval of him. It was in such marked contrast to the wavering, lukewarm faith that Kinnard had had to contend with recently that he searched for a reason. He wondered if he had found it when he learned that evening that two of the old cows had gone down during the afternoon. Too weak to regain their feet, Buckmaster had shot them. Undoubtedly it had made him realize that others would have to go the same way; that it was foolish to try to save them all. Fear often brought a man to his senses. Possibly it had begun to dawn on him that if they were going to get anywhere it was time for the two of them, Kinnard and he, to pull together.

Poor grass and water, with only dead sage for firewood, didn't make for a comfortable camp. The herd was reluctant to bed down. Kinnard spoke to Travis before he went out for the early shift.

"When you come in, Jim, wake me if I'm asleep. I'll stay out with Steve for an hour or so."

Travis interpreted it the only way he could.

"You got Arnett on your mind, eh?"

"I figure it won't hurt to keep my eyes open," Kinnard answered with a non-committal shrug. "The cows are spooky. It wouldn't take much to stampede them."

The night was still, pleasantly cool again, and bright with moonlight when Travis shook him awake. Portugay was moving around the herd, enjoying a cigarette, when he saw him coming.

"What the hell is he doin' out here?" he snarled.

Thinking fast, he crunched out his cigarette. It was almost midnight; Arnett and a couple of his men might be showing up any minute.

"What's wrong?" he demanded suspiciously, as Kinnard rode up.

"Nothing wrong, Steve. With another outfit sitting on our tail, I thought it wouldn't hurt none if I came out with you for an hour or two."

"Okay, if that's how you feel." Portugay was saying the only thing he felt he could say. His first concern was for himself, not for Arnett. If someone stubbed his toe tonight, he meant to see that it was not he.

"Do you want to stay over here and have me circle back to the other side?" he inquired.

It sounded innocent enough. It had not occurred to Kinnard that the horses were in any danger. They were still on their feet foraging for grass. The cows were down.

"That'll be all right, Steve."

It put the little man to the north, near the horses. With the night so bright and Kinnard not so far away, he was convinced that any attempt to run them tonight must not only fail but result in some messy complications. With that in mind, he kept his attention on the rolling, rather broken country to the north, believing that was the direction from which Arnett would move in.

His first thought was to fire three or four shots in the air as soon as he caught a glimpse of them. The shooting would serve a double purpose; it would warn Arnett that something had gone wrong and that the game was off for tonight, and to Kinnard it would come as an alarm.

"Better wait a bit and give 'em a chance to work in before I start bangin' away," he decided. "That'll give me a better story to tell."

His nerves got jumpy as midnight passed and the minutes continued to tick away in a monotonous parade without anything untoward happening to mar their tranquility. At intervals, he met Kinnard. They exchanged a word or two, no more, and circled back around the herd. It got to be one o'clock. If Arnett was going to put in an appearance, he was taking his time about it.

Portugay was about ready to conclude that all this had been much ado about nothing, when a movement to the north caught his eye. Briefly, three riders stood skylined on a little ridge, studying the lay of the land ahead of them. They came off the ridge then, moving slowly and carefully, and quickly disappeared from view. Portugay took it for granted that a gulch or little valley ran along at the base of the ridge and that they were making use of it to get within striking distance of the horses without being seen.

Without changing position, he stood up in the stirrups and scrutinized the open plain, trying to determine where the three riders would reappear. To the east, in the direction of the sand hills, the rolling country offered no concealment. To his left, however, and not more than two hundred and fifty yards away, a limestone outcropping thrust its ragged head into the air. Whether it marked the mouth of the gulch that ran along at the base of the ridge, he couldn't determine. But it struck him that it must be. His attention riveted on it.

He wasn't kept waiting long. He blinked his eyes at first glimpse of them, but it wasn't an illusion; there they were, the three of them, shadowy figures in the moonlight. He didn't hesitate. Throwing a warning yell to Kinnard, he brought his gun up and shattered the stillness of the night with his shooting. Reloading quickly, he flashed away from the herd at a driving gallop. Only when he heard Kinnard pounding up behind him, did he swing off toward the limestone outcropping.

"What the hell is it?" Kinnard yelled.

"Hoss thieves! Three of 'em!"

Riding recklessly, he led the way up the gulch. He knew there was nothing to fear there; the three men had understood the meaning of his warning shots and were long gone. He was watching the ridge. In three or four minutes, he saw them on their way up. With the expertness of an accomplished rider, he pulled his horse to a frantic stop that had the animal pawing the air.

"There they go, Kinnard!" he yelled, pointing at the crest of the ridge. He used his gun again.

Kinnard caught a fleeting glimpse of the three riders.

"Save your ammunition," he advised, his voice raw with vexation. "Shooting is meaningless now. You start talking. I want to know what happened."

Portugay had his story ready.

"Horse thieves, you think, eh?" Kinnard questioned pityingly. "You ought to know better than that, Steve. Even an Indian, who knows all there is to know about lifting horses, wouldn't try it on a night as bright as this. We can chalk this job up to Arnett."

The shooting had aroused the camp. Buckmaster and Ike Jarvis were the first to reach him.

"Steve can tell you more about it than I can," said he. For reasons of his own, he wanted the little man to do the talking.

Portugay told his story without tripping himself. Since Kinnard had been riding guard with him, he could not, as he had hoped, throw any blame on him for what had happened. He glanced at Kinnard, expecting him to mention Arnett. Instead, the latter said guilelessly:

"We were lucky, at that. After this, we'll double guard at night. I don't like to do it, it'll mean less sleep for all hands, but it'll cut down the chances of our being raided again."

At the wagon he sat down with Jamie and her father. If he had been reticent before, he spoke freely now.

"Arnett was behind this," he said bluntly. "There's no other way to look at it."

"I can't believe it," she protested skeptically. "You're letting your dislike of the man run away with you, Frank. You can't seriously think that Worth would stoop to stealing our horses."

"No, he wasn't interested in stealing them—just stampeding them into the sand hills and giving us a day's work rounding them up. And I'll tell you something else, Jamie: I don't like Steve's part in this business. He's an experienced man; he knew where I was; if he'd come around to me instead of banging away with his gun and scaring them off, we might have done something."

"He saved the horses—"

"And that satisfies you, eh? You don't believe we should have done something to discourage that bunch from having another try at it?"

Hot anger was flashing through him and he was not in a mood to check it.

"Seems that every time I have anything to say against Portugay, you're quick to defend him," he ran on. "He's got around you, sure enough. I hope you don't regret it."

He had never used that tone to her before. She was not slow to resent it.

"You're being insufferable now," she retorted, her lips white with indignation. "Steve's a hard worker, he's always agreeable—"

"You're entitled to your opinion, Jamie. It doesn't change mine. I don't trust him. If I could find a man to take his place, I'd fire him in a minute."

7

In the morning, Kinnard looked the stock over carefully, especially the old cows, before he went to the wagon for breakfast. Their condition was such that, having had a look at the arid country through which they were to be driven that day, he felt reasonably certain that a decision as to their fate would have to be reached before evening. Even at that early hour the air was dry and warm. He mentioned it to Buckmaster as the latter came over with his cup and plate and sat down beside him.

"Warm ain't the word for it," said Jesse, with a humorless grunt. "She's going to be hot. Nothin' unusual about that for northern Oklahoma this time of year. Thank God, there's little or no wind to lick up what little moisture there is."

Kinnard had never professed to have any acquaintance with the country below the Nebraska line. It has been Buckmaster's contention that any tenderfoot could find the way into Kansas just by following his nose. That was what Kinnard had been doing up to now. Knowing that there was no water and little grass for the next eight miles to the north, he advised striking off to the northwest, as he had seen old Cimmaron Smith do.

"I was over that way for three or four miles yesterday, Jesse. I found a pond like this one, but dry. What there is beyond it, I don't know. If he's as well acquainted with this country as Jim Travis says he is, I'm willing to believe there's water somewhere in that direction. You'll see the trail Arnett's outfit made. Just tell Jamie to follow it. If I have any luck, I'll be back about noon."

Following the trail Arnett had left took him in the direction of the dried-up pond he had seen the previous day. As he neared it, he saw tracks going to it, the tracks of a single horse. He reasoned that Cim Smith had gone in to have a look at the pond. The herd had not stopped there. It encouraged him in the belief that the old scout knew where there was water ahead. Without hesitating, he continued to follow the cattle droppings and the tire marks Arnett's wagons had made.

An hour's riding brought him to a long, winding valley, running north and south, at the bottom of which flowed a meandering stream, fringed here and there with clumps of cottonwood. As he sat there looking it over carefully before he came down the slope, it became crystal clear to him that Arnett, knowing good grass and water were to be found here, had had no purpose in mind in trying to grab the disputed pond other than to make trouble for him.

Coming down to the creek, he saw where Arnett's herd had bedded. Picking up the trail they left this morning, he followed it for several miles. Cimmaron Smith was staying close to the stream. Whenever he got away from it for a few hundred yards it was only to save time by cutting across a bend. Kinnard saw nothing of the outfit. When he was convinced that it was moving along well ahead of him, he turned back.

Buoyed up by the good news he was carrying (it was better than he knew), Kinnard lost no time in returning to the herd. He expected to find that it had covered some four miles in his absence. He was a good judge of distance. He had marked an imaginary spot in his mind. When he reached it, the outfit wasn't even in sight. Riding up a swell on the prairie floor, he saw it stalled, half a mile away. By the way the cattle had spread out, looking for grass, he knew it had been there sometime. He could see Honey walking around the wagon, whip in hand and flicking it disgustedly at the surrounding sage-brush. The men and Jamie were gathered together in a tight little knot some distance away. He needed no more to tell him that something was decidedly amiss.

It took him only a few minutes to reach the wagon. As he swept past it, he saw that Jamie and the men were gathered around her father. They saw him coming and she ran out to meet him.

"What's the trouble?" he demanded anxiously, as he swung down.

"Frank, we're up against it. The old cows simply won't go on. They just stand there with their eyes rolling and sides heaving like they'd drop any moment. The boys—even Ike—insist there's nothing to do but destroy them."

He had never seen her so distraught. With the hardness gone from his voice, he said:

"You got to pull yourself together, Jamie. You wouldn't admit it, but you knew as well as I that it would come to this . . . What's your father got to say?"

"It's unnerved him. He knows it must be done, but he can't bring himself to say so. You can understand, Frank—"

"Of course. I'll talk to him."

"If you can give him a little encouragement—something to buck him up—I'll be eternally grateful. I know this isn't the end of the world; that we'll go on. But he's so discouraged."

"I'll do my best," he promised. "You keep your chin up."

Ike Jarvis and Portugay stepped aside to make room for him as he joined the circle. Jesse Buckmaster gave him a dejected, head-hanging glance. Ignoring it, Kinnard said:

"We got good water and grass about eight miles west of us, Jesse. Plenty wood. Just about the nicest country we've seen since leaving home."

"That's good," Buckmaster responded tonelessly, his mood as dark and melancholy as ever. "It could be the Garden of Eden and it wouldn't matter to some of my stuff. This is as far as they can go."

Kinnard had never seen him looking so old and worn. His grizzled face was lined and cavernous beneath his beard.

"I reckon you just been waitin' me out, Kinnard," he went on. There was no animosity in his tone. "You knew the time would come when I couldn't close my eyes to what's wrong with this outfit any longer. I'm speakin' about my old cows. I shoulda taken your advice before we started out and sold 'em for whatever I could git. I'd put too much sweat and worryin' into buildin' a herd around them to let them go for a song. Now I can leave their carcasses here for the wolves to feed on."

He had more to say, all in the same vein. Kinnard's gorge began to rise. Having to destroy the old cows was regrettable, but to magnify it into a major calamity, as Jesse was doing, was, to him, an unconscious exhibition of weakness. He knew that, deep down, there was iron in the man. There was no reason to believe that it would be brought to the surface by sympathizing with him. Disregarding his promise to Jamie, he took a firm stand with her father.

"Jesse, I'm not going to listen to any more of this nonsense. You didn't expect to reach Montana without losing some stock. We'll be lucky to get there with seventy-five per cent of what we started out with. The old stuff has been a drag on us for days. Getting rid of it will give the rest of the herd a better chance. That's the only way to look at it."

"I reckon it is," the old man mumbled. "God knows I want to do what's best for us. You got to give me a little time."

"No, we're not going to waste any more time," Kinnard said adamantly. "I know what's got to be done and I'll do it. Ike, you and Steve go back with me; I want the rest of you to get the outfit moving. We'll catch up with you."

Jamie pushed past her father and faced him, her eyes flashing with reckless anger.

"We don't have to dance to your dictation!" she cried. "Don't you dare to shoot those cows without Dad's permission!"

She had visited her anger on him on more than one previous occasion but he had never seen her give way to her emotion in such wild, impassioned fury as this. It made him realize as never before how strong the bond was between her and her father. But as far as this matter was concerned, he was at the end of his patience with both.

"It's no longer a question of permission," he said sternly. "I'm going to do what should have been done days ago."

She started to take a step after him as he walked away, but her father caught her arm and stopped her.

"Let him go, Jamie. We'll have no argument

about it. What he says is true; it's got to be done. You tell Honey to get the wagon rollin'. The rest of us will push the stock along. I want to git away from here and the sooner the better."

Out of respect for the feelings of the Buckmasters, Kinnard waited until the plodding herd was more than half a mile away before he permitted the first shot to be fired. Shooting helpless cows was a grisly business. It was as repugnant to old Ike as it was to him; only Portugay seemed to find an obscure pleasure in it.

The slaughter continued and though the late morning was hot and still, faint telltale puffs of sound reached Jamie and her father. He steeled himself against looking back. She tried to be equally resolute, but as the firing continued, she glanced back against her will and felt suddenly ill as she saw the stiffening carcasses that littered the plain.

It seemed to be a long time before Kinnard and the others rejoined the outfit. The former rode ahead to the wagon. After speaking to Honey for a minute, he dropped back to Jamie and her father.

"I told Honey to hold off on dinner till we reach the creek," he informed them. "The way we're moving along now, we'll be there by the middle of the afternoon. We'll put up for the night at the first good spot we find."

Jamie's response was limited to a frigid nod.

Giving him her place, she dropped back to ride swing with Steve. She shuddered as she thought of the weeks ahead, forced to dance to his tune. But to resent the authority he gave himself was one thing; to do something about it was another. That what he did was so often right made his superior air no less unpalatable.

She remembered how opposed he had been to having her accompany the drive. That once, at least, he had been compelled to give in. But he had attached a string to it; when they reached Ellsworth it would be up to him to decide whether she was to go on.

"We'll have something to say about that," she promised herself. "This is our crew, not his. He can take his cows and go his own way!"

Angry though she was, the thought no sooner flashed across her mind than she realized how rash it was; they needed Kinnard and he needed them. The invisible chains of circumstance and dire necessity would hold them together as securely as though they were forged of steel.

She was doing a man's work, and doing it well. He could find no fault with her on that score. Though the work was hard, she had stood up to it, and without receiving or asking for any special consideration on account of her sex. But it was no life for a woman. She had no privacy and none of the little refinements that so recently had been hers. She never complained. Secretly, however, she found doing without them harder to bear than the physical discomforts she endured daily.

She had had the feeling lately that Kinnard often went out of his way deliberately to ignore her. She didn't know what his reasons were; but as she watched him now, up ahead, riding point with her father, she searched her mind for a way to humble him. But that seemed impossible. It did occur to her, however, that if she couldn't humble him she might infuriate him by being increasingly friendly with Steve Portugay. She knew how he felt about Steve. She had known a hundred cowpunchers like the little man with the flashing teeth. Maybe he wasn't reliable, but she refused to believe he was dangerous. She was confident she could handle him.

"After all," she reflected, "I'm no child. I'll give him just a little encouragement and we'll see what Mr. Frank Kinnard makes of it!"

They reached the creek in mid-afternoon. Short of another mile, they found an excellent place to bed down the herd and make camp. It was the earliest they had stopped in days. Even so, and in spite of the delay, they had done better than ten miles.

"We'll do fifteen tomorrow," Kinnard assured Buckmaster.

Gathering up a towel and an armful of clothes that badly needed washing, Jamie went to the creek. She moved along the shallow bank until she was several hundred yards down the little stream. When she had finished with the clothes and hung them up to dry, she undressed and waded into the water. The pool was deep enough for swimming. Though she couldn't swim a stroke, it was refreshing just to be in the water.

Portugay had seen her leave camp. His curiosity was aroused when he observed how much distance she was putting between herself and the wagon. A few clothes could be washed anywhere. It didn't take him long to surmise her intention. Slipping off, he followed her. He was not fifty yards away, screened by the brush, when she stepped out on the bank and stood there drying herself.

His senses rocked and reason began to run out of him as he stared at her, with her firm young breasts, her slim, rounded body so feminine and so desirable. As he crouched in the brush, gasping for breath in his eagerness, voices sounded behind him. It was Jim Travis and Johnny, coming down for a swim. Realizing that he was about to be trapped, he began tearing off his clothes that he might make it appear that his intentions were as innocent as theirs.

"There's a good pool over here!" he called to them.

Embarrassed to discover that she wasn't alone, Jamie snatched up her clothes and darted behind a clump of young willows. Dressing hurriedly she picked her way through the trees and brush to the open prairie.

The long hot day began to draw to a close as they sat around eating dinner. The air was cooling off already. Honey, not pressed for time this once, had outdone himself. Not having eaten since five that morning, they were ravenous. Honey's round black face beamed as they cleaned their plates and came back for second helpings.

"Missy, ah ain't seen you eatin' like this since we left home," he told Jamie. "It shore does me good. Mebbe I'll have a special treat for you tomorrow night—that's if yo're still fond of razzberry pie."

"You know that's one of my weaknesses, Honey. I thought of it soon as I saw those wild berries growing along the creek."

"You'll have yore pie, missy. I'll pick a panful and stew 'em up this evenin'."

"If you'll bake the pie, Honey, I'll pick the berries," she laughed. "Let me have a pan."

Portugay had overheard the exchange. He popped to his feet at once.

"I'll be glad to give you a hand, mam," he offered.

She knew Kinnard was listening. Surmising that he wouldn't like it, she said with a grateful little smile:

"Thank you, Steve. Let's get started."

Kinnard dissembled whatever displeasure he

felt, and it was considerable, as they walked away. He sat where he was, but through the smoke of his cigarette he watched them as they moved in and out among the raspberry vines. They were seldom out of sight for more than a few minutes at a time. He expected that they would work either up or down the creek and away from camp. But they didn't. He found it so enlightening that a half-amused smile ruffled his lips. He felt that they remained where they could be seen from the wagon by design and not by accident. He was equally sure it was Jamie's doing, not what Steve wanted.

Portugay's intentions in regard to her were no puzzle to Kinnard. The man had a savage, animal-like ferocity that had a certain appeal for some women. But he was crude and ignorant and obvious. Though Kinnard had some reason to know how incalculable human beings were, he was convinced that Steve Portugay could never interest her. In fact, he found it easy to believe that she was not the least bit in the dark about the man.

Kinnard drew a sort of sardonic satisfaction from the thought. The only conclusion he could reach was that Jamie was playing a game. That she meant it to be at his expense was unescapable.

"Playing with that pup was just a trick to steam me up," he thought. "The little fool can get over her head before she knows it."

When Jamie and Portugay returned from their berry picking, Kinnard appeared as indifferent as though he hadn't noticed that they had ever left the wagon. Going to his horse, he went out to have a look at the stock. It had been watered, but it was on good grass and showed no inclination to bed down yet.

He was surprised to see Jesse standing up on the wagon seat, staring off to the south, when he came back.

"What is it?" he asked at once.

"Another outfit comin' up the valley. You'll see 'em when they come out of that swale a mile or so to the south."

The wagons, two of them, caught his eye first. He saw the point men and the herd itself a few moments later. The big crew handling it had it moving right along for so late in the day, and without stragglers.

"They're going to pass close to us," said Kinnard. "Saddle up; we'll throw a ring around our stuff. You stay close to me, Jesse, till we find out what their intentions are."

They were in position in good time to hold their stock where it was.

"That's a good-lookin' outfit," Jesse commented. The point men had swung out to pass them at a safe distance. It stilled whatever apprehension he had felt. "Somethin' familiar about that big fella ridin' left point."

The man in question now left the drive and came loping toward them. Buckmaster recognized him.

"It's Nick Brewster of 44."

Kinnard had heard Brewster and the big 44 outfit mentioned so often that he was not unacquainted with the man's prominence.

"So it's you, Jesse!" Brewster sounded surprised. He was a big, florid-faced man with a booming voice. "I didn't know you was ahead of us. We'll swing around you and go up the creek a mile or better and be out of your way in the mornin'."

Jesse made him acquainted with Kinnard. The big man favored the latter with an approving nod.

"I've heard of you. I didn't know you was acquainted with the country around here."

"I'm not," Kinnard admitted frankly. "I've never seen it before. That goes for Jesse, too."

"Then you're doin' all right for greenhorns. This is Cottonwood Creek. It's the best way north. Stay with it for about seventy-five miles and you can't go wrong. When you finally have to leave it, you won't be more'n another seventy-five from the Arkansaw."

"You figger you may have trouble gittin' your stuff acrost, Nick?" Jesse inquired.

"No, not this late in the year. But you never can be sure of that dang river. It all depends on what's been goin' on hundreds of miles away in

113

the Rockies . . . You got anybody ahead of you, Jesse?"

"Yeh, Arnett. He drove through here yesterday. He's got Cim Smith with him."

"Yeh, I knew," Brewster grunted, and suddenly his affability disappeared. "We got too much stuff to trail it in one bunch. I got three herds comin' up. I wanted Cim to take one. It was all set till Arnett got the old man likkered up and stole him away from me."

As he talked he watched the progress of his outfit.

"I aim to remember it," he continued. "It was a dirty, underhanded business. Seems like you can't tell who's goin' to cut your throat next. Those bastards in Washington sure had a good try at it, but I still got my chin up." He glanced over his shoulder again. "I got to be catchin' up now. I may see you tomorrow evenin' in Kansas."

"We that near the line?" Kinnard inquired.

"Yeh, just a few miles."

The news cheered Buckmaster.

"We ain't doin' so bad," he declared.

"We'll do better from now on," Kinnard said confidently.

For the first time they did fifteen miles the next day, and as they went up the valley of the Cottonwood they maintained that pace. It had an encouraging effect on Jesse and he began to feel compensated for the loss of the old cows. His moodiness disappeared, and around the fire in the evening he spoke optimistically of their chances of getting through to Montana before August was gone.

They saw nothing of Arnett and on only one occasion were they near enough Nick Brewster's outfit to induce Kinnard and Jesse to ride over and spend an hour with him.

Jamie continued to play what she considered her innocent game with Steve Portugay. She was sure that Kinnard's indifference was strained and false and that, though he pretended otherwise, he secretly watched every move she made. It pleased her to believe that beneath his smiling, half-contemptuous unconcern he was getting ready to explode.

It had started with the killing of the old cows. That no longer mattered; she wanted to hurt him, punish him in some way. She didn't ask herself why. If she had, the answer would have eluded her. A dozen times a day she told herself he could never mean anything to her. And yet he was seldom out of her thoughts for long. But with peculiar feminine perversity she closed her eyes to such inconsistencies. Nor did she give any consideration to what effect her advances were having on Steve Portugay. To her he was just a necessary pawn. But she had given him no reason to think so. It had lighted a fire in him that was rapidly getting out of control. On their fourth night on the Cottonwood it burst out in consuming flame.

The wagon was drawn up within a few feet of the creek and some distance from the dying fire. It was ten o'clock. It had become the rule to double guard the stock. Ike Jarvis and Johnny were out, standing the first watch. The rest of the camp was asleep, when it was aroused by Jamie's piercing scream.

Kinnard popped up in his blankets to see her, scantily clad, bolt out from beneath the wagon, pushing Portugay away. Snatching Honey's whip out of the socket, she lashed out viciously at him, cutting him back and forth across the face. The long stock whip was heavy and every blow she struck wrung a grunt out of her.

"Damn you!" she cried, gasping for breath. "I'll mark you good for that!"

Steve stood there taking a beating, not knowing what else to do. With the camp watching him, he couldn't run for it or strike her.

Kinnard had paused only long enough to pull on his boots. Reaching her, he wrested the whip out of her hands.

"Now stand back and answer me," he commanded, "What did he do?"

"Why, the crazy fool tried to crawl into the blankets with me!" She was so beside herself that it was difficult for her to speak. "What does he think I am? If I—"

"That's enough," Kinnard cut her off, a controlled anger thinning his face. "You been asking for this. I don't blame Steve half as much as I do you. What did you expect him to think? He didn't know you were only fooling."

"How dare you?" she cried, a stricken look in her eyes. "You—you—" she couldn't finish it. "Don't you tell me I'm cheap—"

"Not cheap, just silly, Jamie. I warned you that little girls who play with fire often get their fingers burnt, but you wouldn't listen."

Out of the corner of his eye Kinnard saw her father rush at Portugay, gun in hand. He caught him by the arm and held him back.

"Stop where you are, Jesse. This nonsense has gone far enough. Steve made a mistake, but no harm's been done."

"By God, he'll apologize—"

"He'll apologize."

"I lost my head," Portugay muttered, wiping his bleeding chin with the back of his hand. "I'm sorry."

"All right," Kinnard said with authority, "we'll say no more about it and let it go at that. It's time for you and Lin to be going out for the second shift, Steve. The rest of you go back to sleep."

It left the three of them alone. Jamie had turned to her father. Kinnard could hear her crying as she buried her head on Jesse's shoulder. He had not expected tears from her. It shook him, but there was little forbearance in him tonight.

"I don't know what the upshot of this will be," said he. "It puts us in an awkward spot with Portugay. I don't like the man, I don't trust him; and as I told Jamie the other day, I'd hand him his time in a minute if we could replace him. But we can't; and we need him. Now the shoe is on the other foot, I'm afraid. Instead of giving him his time, he'll most likely be asking for it. He was horse-whipped in front of the rest of the crew. Usually a man doesn't try to live down a thing like that; he just runs. We got to try to hold on to him, Jesse."

"What do you want me to do, Kinnard?"

"Talk to the men. You're closer to them than I am. Tell them to lay off Portugay, that you don't want any talk."

Jamie looked up, her eyes wet with her tears.

"Frank, I've been awfully foolish. You know what I was trying to do—"

"No, I don't, and I'm not interested in finding out," he returned, more concerned with concealing his own feelings than in hurting hers.

"Then I suppose this means that you're not taking me beyond Ellsworth—"

"You haven't left me much choice, have you, Jamie?"

"Please, Frank!" she pleaded.

She was a picture as she stood there in her flimsy nightgown, her hair disheveled, her bare arms and shoulders smooth and white in the moonlight, her eyes brimming over. She had never appealed to him more.

"I won't give you an answer tonight," he told her, the sternness of his voice an effort. "We'll see when the time comes. Whatever I do will have to be for the good of the outfit."

8

Steve Portugay's thoughts were murderous as he kept his lonely watch. He was always predisposed to resort to violence and hatred to avenge a wrong, real or fancied. It relieved him very little to pour out his venom on Jamie. The whipping he had received was nothing in itself. But the crew had witnessed it, and it was that, the loss of face, that made him writhe with ignominy. For that, he hated the lot of them, and Kinnard most of all. It didn't matter that Kinnard had absolved him; he hated him for a score of reasons. He damned Arnett too.

"If it wasn't for the deal he made with me, I'd have cut loose from this goddamn outfit weeks ago!"

He'd cut loose from it now, and to hell with Arnett. He was set on that. But he cooled down as he continued moving around the herd and midnight passed. After all, money was money. If he ran out on Arnett now, he'd get no more.

"He ain't more'n a day ahead of us," he reflected. "He said he'd cross the Arkansaw at Bidler's Station. We ought to catch him there."

On that chance, he decided he'd hang on with Kinnard until then, collect what he could from Arnett and ride west to Dodge.

Kinnard and Buckmaster saw to it that there

was no laughing at the little man's expense, at least not to his face. Though he was sullen and uncommunicative, he did his work well. It was noticeable that he went out of his way to avoid Jamie. She was equally reticent. She no longer sat around with the crew in the evening as they left the Cottonwood and struck north for the Arkansas.

Kinnard made no overtures to her even when he was satisfied that she was a genuinely chastened young woman. He found it increasingly difficult as the days ran on to ignore her and be ignored in turn. Several times he was at the point of breaking down and trying to patch up their differences. When they made what he meant to be their last camp before reaching the river, he gave her an opening. She refused to take it. It gave him a bad moment, and he turned away wondering if the rift between them had become so deep that it could never be healed.

A surprise awaited them when they reached the Arkansas. It was in flood, running bank full. Four outfits were piled up there, waiting to get across; 44, Arnett and two others. Kinnard saw that there was nothing to do but move back from the river, as the others were doing, and turn the stock out to grass.

Nick Brewster rode into camp during the afternoon. Though he would never see sixty again, he was still all fight.

"We don't seem to be able to shake our bad luck," he growled. "Had all our hurryin' for nothin'."

"How long do you figger we'll be held up here, Nick?" Jesse inquired.

"Two or three days. Must be a lot of snow goin' off up in the Rockies all at once. That's Joe Black's outfit off there to the west. The damn fool tried to put some stuff across. It got swept away before it got thirty feet from the bank. You seen anythin' of Arnett?"

"No—"

"He's keepin' away from me. I'm on my way down to Jake's place now. Always stopped for a drink or two whenever we was drivin' beef up to Abilene."

He was referring to Jake Bidler, who ran a saloon and grocery a mile below the crossing. Jake refused to believe that the recently confirmed state law banning the sale of intoxicating beverages was really a law. He had a lot of company.

"I'll go down with you," Kinnard said. "I'm running short of tobacco."

They found half a dozen men, owners and punchers from the stalled herds, gathered there. The high water was a windfall for Bidler and he was making the most of it. He remembered Brewster and after they had exchanged a few words he set up the drinks. Brewster returned the courtesy and so did Kinnard. They were standing at the bar—it was just a pineboard counter—some minutes later when Worth Arnett walked in. He seemed to know that Brewster was there. If he was surprised to find him in Kinnard's company, he failed to let it make any difference to him. Ignoring the latter, he knocked the glass out of the old man's hand and swung him around.

Kinnard has seen the tall man enraged before but never more than now.

"I'm going to cram the lying talk you been spreading about me right down your throat, Brewster!" Arnett whipped out fiercely. "You may be the biggest man in Oklahoma, but that cuts no ice with me. You're a goddamn liar when you say I got Cim Smith drunk and stole him away from you."

"That's what you did," Brewster flung back defiantly.

"You mean I offered him three times as much money as you wanted to give him. If he got likkered up it wasn't till after I had his name on a piece of paper."

"And I say you're a liar!" Brewster thundered. For a man who hadn't worn a gun in years, he wasn't backing down an inch. "The only time you ever shoot square with a man is when you can't find a way to cheat him."

With a snarl of insane rage Arnett raised his gun and pistol-whipped the old man. The first blow of the heavy .44 laid Brewster's scalp open. Arnett hit him a second time and a third. With blood spurting from his slashed forehead Brewster crumpled to the floor, unconscious.

It had happened so quickly that Bidler and the others stood rooted in their tracks. Before they could find their tongues, or do anything for Brewster, Kinnard waved them back. Facing Arnett, he said with wicked contempt:

"Is that the best you can do, Arnett—gun-whipping an unarmed man who's old enough to be your grandfather?"

There was a challenge in his talk that flattened against Arnett. He understood it, and so did every man in the store, save Nick Brewster. He knew a moment's wavering between desire and discretion but the black hatred he bore Kinnard would not let him retreat.

"You goddamn Yankee, I don't need no gun to put you on the floor. I can do that with my bare fists."

"All right, hand your gun to Bidler; I'll do the same." Kinnard's quiet, composed tone had something in it that tightened the nerves of those who heard him. "A couple of you men pick Nick up and see if you can't stop that bleeding."

He didn't rate himself better than fair with his fists. Whenever possible he had avoided saloon brawling; but this once, however it went, he was eager for it. In height and reach Arnett had all the advantage. As he had observed him, however, he was not a quick-moving man. To win, Kinnard knew he had to keep moving and manage to come up under those long arms.

Arnett was moving toward him then, slightly crouched, his fists knotted and held close to his body, ready to lash out with either hand. Brewster had been placed in an old chair that Bidler kept in the place for his own comfort. It had been pushed back to make more room. It still left only a long narrow space extending from the bar to the door. Believing the only way he could win was to outsmart Arnett and confuse him with the unexpected, he made his first move with that in mind. The space between the bar and the opposite counter was so narrow that he was sure the tall man wouldn't be looking for him to try to slip past and come up in back of him. Maybe it couldn't be done, but Kinnard knew he had to gamble.

With arms cocked, he took a step to the left, telegraphing his intention to swarm in from that side. Fooled by the deception, Arnett let go with a wild, whistling right hand. It put him off balance when his fist landed on nothing but thin air. Kinnard slipped past him to the right, his shoulder driving Arnett aside a step. It gave him elbow room, and as he passed he ripped a punishing blow deep into the other's belly.

It drove the breath out of Arnett with a loud

whoosh and doubled him up in agony. When he turned to find his man, his guard was down momentarily. Before he could get it up an iron fist crashed his chin. It was delivered with force enough to lift him to his toes. He had been so sure how this would go. Now doubt flickered in his eyes. It disappeared when Kinnard came in a second time and he caught him and slashed him across the mouth and sent him reeling back.

And now he had Kinnard where he wanted him, pinned up against the rear wall of the building. With his long arms held wide to prevent the man's escaping, he closed in.

Kinnard charged into him savagely, head lowered and broke up Arnett's bull-like rush. He forced the other to give ground but he took a beating. He couldn't ward off those long flailing arms, nor reach the tall man's face. His own arms were working like pistons as he hammered Arnett around the body. He was hurt now and with the taste of his own blood in his mouth, he fought like an enraged beast.

He was driven to his knees finally, and as Arnett tried to break away, he caught him around the legs and upset him. On the floor, both of them, they glowered at each other like two wounded grizzlies. Slowly they hauled themselves to their feet. Kinnard used his quickness now. Like a human battering ram he flung himself at Arnett, his knees driving him, and carried him toward the open door. The tall man's legs got tangled up and as he stumbled Kinnard had an open shot at his face.

Both men were tiring, but here was an opening that might not come again. Kinnard had enough strength left to take advantage of it. Risking everything on one blow, he caught Arnett with a crashing right hand that exploded just under the cheekbone. The tall Texan's head snapped back and struck the door frame with a resounding thud. The flimsy building shook with the impact. This double punishment jarred Arnett loose from his senses. A glazed look came into his eyes and he slumped to his knees. He reached out in vain for the other's legs as he went down. Kinnard kicked his hands aside and stepped back, waiting for him to get up.

Arnett covered his face with his hands, expecting Kinnard to use his boots on him, as he would have done had the situation been reversed. This sort of fighting had no rules; you maimed your man anyway you could. When he realized that he wasn't to be booted into unconsciousness, contempt for the other's weakness twisted his battered mouth. Seeing he was safe as long as he stayed on his knees, he took advantage of the respite, drawing deep breaths of air into his heaving lungs. When he was ready, he got up and struck out with wild, swinging blows. But the power had gone out of his long arms.

Kinnard no longer had to stay away from him. He could stay in close now and reach that battered face almost at will.

They fought and heaved senselessly until their strength was spent. Their legs were uncertain. They began to stumble blindly. Arnett took a clumsy backward step. Kinnard lunged at him. It swept Arnett off his feet. Clinging together, they plunged through the open door and sprawled in the dust, rolling apart as they struck the ground.

The onlookers poured out of the store and stood watching. They saw Kinnard struggle to his feet. Arnett tried to get up, but he couldn't make it. Two men, one on either side, took Kinnard by the arm and led him to the steps and sat him down. From the doorway, Bidler said:

"Douse him with a bucket of water. I'll get some whisky."

This standard frontier medication had the desired effect. Kinnard's head cleared and his mind began to function.

"You don't look purty, but I reckon yo're all right," Bidler told him, with coarse good humor.

"What about Nick Brewster?" Kinnard asked.

"He's groggy but he'll be okay. I got his head bound up." He paused to gaze at Arnett. "Better give him a dousin', boys, and put him on his horse. I'll hand you his gun."

Kinnard went inside. Brewster was able to talk.

"Thank you, son," the big man said. "If I'd had

a gun on me I'd have killed that tinhorn and then regretted it the rest of my life. But there was no call for you to take up my quarrel."

"What I did wasn't all on your account, Nick. I had a score of my own to settle with that party. If you think you can sit in your saddle, I'll take you back to your outfit."

Brewster had a roundup cook who was also something of a buckshot surgeon. He spent half an hour administering to the old man before he turned his attention to Kinnard.

"I'll see what I can do for you now," said he.

"Don't bother. I'm cut up a little, that's all."

"You wouldn't talk that way if you could see yourself, son," Brewster contradicted. "The least we can do is wash you up and give you a clean shirt. You don't want to go back to your wagon and have the girl see you lookin' like that."

Kinnard hadn't given any thought to facing Jamie. Now that he did, he allowed himself to be persuaded. But a clean shirt and what Brewster's cook was able to do for him couldn't conceal the fact that he had been in a fight. Jamie knew it the moment she saw his puffed and lacerated face. The shock of it leveled the barrier of aloofness and unconcern she had raised against him.

"Frank, you've been fighting!" she cried, her eyes brimming with solicitude.

"Yeh, down the river at the store. I had a fight with Arnett."

"Did you lick him?" she demanded, smothering a little gasp of surprise. Her tone was so urgent and plainly partisan to him that he had to smile, painful as it was.

"I didn't think it mattered to you—"

"Answer me!" she insisted.

"I licked him. He had words with Brewster and gun-whipped him—"

"And that was all the excuse you needed. I suppose." Her tone was unconsciously accusing. He gave her a closer look.

"Are you finding fault with me now? I needed no excuse; he's been in my hair a long time. Slugging an unarmed man with his gun just confirmed my long-held opinion of him. For your sake, I didn't want any trouble with Arnett." He shook his head regretfully. "I'm sorry I let myself go."

"For my sake?" she queried, throwing his words back at him. "What did I have to do with it?"

"Come now, Jamie, you're not that innocent," he rebuked her. "It was taken for granted in Canadian Crossing that you'd be marrying Arnett one day."

"That's very funny," she laughed divertingly. "I used to go to dances with him; he's asked me to marry him many times." Her tone changed and she was suddenly grave. "There was never anything between us, Frank. You come over to the wagon with me. I'm going to bathe your face with Epsom salts. It'll reduce the swelling and help heal the cuts."

Soaking a cloth pad in the warm solution she had prepared, she went over his face tenderly, dabbing the abrasions.

"I know it stings a bit," she said as she felt him wince.

"It doesn't amount about to anything," he assured her. To have her ministering to him was such a pleasant experience that it far outweighed the contingent stabs of pain.

When she was finished, she sat down beside him on the wagon tongue. They talked freely and without any trace of self-consciousness, their feuding of the past week forgotten.

"It's good to hear you laughing again," he said. "I've been wearing too long a face myself. Maybe things will be different after we get across."

He had noticed that they were quiet. He could see her father and Ike Jarvis out with the herd. No one else seemed to be around, not even Honey. He asked about them.

"They're often visiting. This is the first chance they've had to talk to anyone in weeks. I suppose most of them will go down to the store for a few drinks. Dad warned them not to come back likkered up." She frowned as she gazed off toward the river. "I hope we won't be held up here too long. I don't want you to have any more trouble with Worth."

"I can think of a better reason for getting across," he said thoughtfully. "Another outfit pulled in in back of 44 this noon. More will be showing up. There'll be so many cows here before long that it will be like turning loose a horde of grasshoppers on this section of Kansas when they're let go. Brewster and I had some talk about it. It might be wise to change our plans some and head off in the direction of Abilene and pass to the east of Ellsworth instead of the west."

"That means adding a lot of extra miles, Frank."

"I know it, but it might pay off at that. I believe Brewster is right when he says that most of these Kansas men wouldn't get up on their ear when a trail herd uses their water. They don't have too much beyond their own needs. What riles them is to have one outfit after another grabbing it."

"Is Mr. Brewster going up east of Ellsworth?"

"He is. He'll soon pull ahead of us; we can't travel as fast as he can. I don't mean we should trail along after 44; but I'm for striking off in that general direction. I'm going to talk it over with your father."

Until a few weeks ago, she had never heard of Ellsworth, Kansas. Though it was a place of little consequence, it had become to her of the greatest importance. Of late, whenever she heard it mentioned, it seemed to her that it was a sword hanging over her head, and she had come to hate the sound of it. To hear him speak of it now sent a little shiver down her spine. But she found the courage to question him.

"After we get across the Arkansas, Frank, how long will it take us to reach Ellsworth?"

"Four, five days," he replied, sensing instantly what was on her mind.

"If I have to leave the outfit," she went on resolutely, "I imagine I can take a train there that will take me east to the Missouri. I could go up the river by steamboat."

"You could. But that won't be necessary." He made it sound impersonal, knowing no other way in which to conceal the extent of his surrender.

"Well!" she gasped. It had come so suddenly that momentarily she was at a loss for words. And then, in a small hushed voice, she said: "That takes a load off my mind!"

"And mine, too." He got to his feet. "You got nothing to worry about."

Settling his Stetson firmly on his head, he started to walk away. She caught his arm and stopped him.

"Frank—I want to thank you."

"No need to. As I told you before, I got to regard you as just a member of the crew. On those terms, you deserve it."

Their eyes met and held. The impulse to take her in his arms began to run away with him. He steeled himself against it.

"I suppose there'll always be a tug of war between us; you'll see things one way and I another. But I'll always admire and respect you, Jamie. I swear to God I'll get you to Montana if I have to carry you."

He was gone then. Misty-eyed, she watched him riding out to join her father and Ike. Somehow the world was suddenly brighter and happier, and not only because Ellsworth, Kansas, would soon be no more than a meaningless crossroads on their back trail.

Steve Portugay had just joined a group of men gathered on the river-bank, when a rider came up from Bidler's place with news of what had occurred there. It in no way affected his determination to reach some sort of a settlement with Arnett and then head for Dodge City. He had no difficulty in locating the Texan's outfit. He didn't expect to find him in an amiable mood; but he couldn't afford to wait for a more fortuitous moment.

Though Arnett had been soundly beaten, his face bore fewer marks than Kinnard's. It was the body punishment he had taken that had cut him down. He had an alibi for his defeat. Steve listened to it and wasn't impressed.

"I'd think you was big enough to wipe up the floor with him," he argued. "What the hell ailed you?"

"I told you he wouldn't stand up and fight like a man. All he did was butt me. A couple times he damn near drove his head clear through me. Don't think I didn't give him something to remember! His face looked like it had been through a meat chopper."

He checked himself and glared owlishly at the little man.

"How have things been going between the Buckmasters and Kinnard?" he demanded.

"I don't know, Arnett," Steve grumbled. "One day they seem ready to fly at each other's throat, the next they got everything patched up. I want to git away from that goddamn outfit. That's why I'm here. I want to talk to you. I figger you owe me some money. I want it. I'm goin' to give Dodge City a whirl for a few days."

"Like hell you are!" Arnett said flatly. "You're goin' through with that bunch all the way to Montana. I'll give you another four hundred dollars if you stick it out and do a good job for me. I won't give you another cent now."

Steve shook his head in violent dissent.

"I can't stick it out no longer. I had some trouble with Buckmaster's girl the other night."

"What kind of trouble?"

"That's my business. I don't know what you're gittin' so damn excited about. You used to run around with her, but you was never serious about any woman."

"Steve, you better start talking!" Arnett whipped out menacingly.

"What the hell!" the little man grunted. "I made a pass at her and she used a horsewhip on me—in front of Kinnard and the whole outfit. That's more'n I can take."

"Go on talking, Steve! Did you put your hands on her?"

"It didn't amount to nothin', I tell you. Even Kinnard said so. He blamed her, not me. Why should it mean anythin' to you? She's passed you up for him."

"Why, you little bastard, I ought to gun you for that!" Arnett raged. "I didn't hire you to get fresh with her. What the hell's the matter with you? That girl is a lady—I expect to make her my wife before I'm through!"

He tramped a circle around Portugay until he was exhausted by his seething violence. Out of the ferment in his brain, a thought popped to the surface that stilled his anger; he needed Steve Portugay. Ironically, and for quite a different reason, he could no more afford to get through with him than Kinnard could.

"I said four hundred, Steve. I'll do better than that if you get Kinnard out of my way. That outfit will belong to Jamie someday. I'd like to have it. I'm putting my cards on the table with you. Play along with me and you won't regret it."

Portugay's eyes grew beady with avarice. He

wasn't to be hurried into a decision, however. Arnett was offering him a stake. But promises were only promises.

"All right," he said firmly. "I ain't takin' it all on tick though. If your levellin' with me, give me couple hundred now. I'll wait for the rest."

"It's a deal," the tall man agreed. After he had given him the money, he said: "We'll be here a couple days. I'll see Jamie tomorrow."

"You're crazy," Steve protested. "Kinnard won't like it. Why press your luck?"

"Don't you worry about my luck, mister. I ain't walking wide of that damn Yankee."

9

When morning dawned, the Arkansas was still impassible, but it was dropping. A feeling of optimism ran through the stalled outfits, half a dozen by now, that they would be able to cross in another twenty-four hours. The stock had to be watered. The only way it could be done safely and without confusion was for the various herds to be driven a short distance up or down the river and watched carefully. It consumed most of the morning, and it was not until after dinner that Jesse and Kinnard rode to the 44 camp to discuss the feasibility of using the Abilene trail for forty to fifty miles before swinging north toward Ellsworth. It was during their absence that Arnett surprised Jamie as she sat in the shade of the wagon, knitting a pair of socks.

"Don't get up," he said. "I'll sit down with you."

She straightened up stiffly, fear, as well as indignation, knifing through her.

"Worth, you must be mad, coming here where you know you're not wanted. You're just asking for trouble."

"I had to see you, Jamie. It's been so long." He was not unaware of the dangerous nature of his visit. Seeing that she appreciated it flattered his vanity and filled him with the spurious self-assurance of an actor who is carried away by the swaggering nature of the character he is portraying. "I don't know what you've been hearing about me. Considering the source, I wouldn't expect it to be to my credit."

"It's not what I've heard, it's what you've done that I don't like." She spoke with a cold hostility that penetrated even his tough hide. "If you are here on my account, you're wasting your time, Worth."

"Why else would I be here?" he asked. "You know how I've always felt about you. I ain't going to let Kinnard come between us."

"That's enough of that!" she cried, getting to her feet, her eyes blazing scornfully. "Don't you give yourself any rights with me. I'm not obligated to you in any way. You don't own any part of me. As for Frank Kinnard, I respect him. There's nothing else between us. If there was, it would be none of your business."

He stood up and faced her, unabashed.

"Maybe I'll make it my business."

"I doubt it. You've always been able to deceive yourself with your own boasting, but you've never really fooled anyone else. I think you better go now, Worth."

It made his blood boil to be humbled in such fashion, and especially by her. The only way he could explain it was that she knew something about his scheming with Portugay. Steve wasn't too bright; she might have wormed something out of him without his knowing it. He didn't dare to say anything about it now, no more than he could question her about the whipping she had given the man.

"I'll leave, if that's what you want," he said with an attempt at his usual bluster, "but I ain't going to be run out like a yellow cur with my tail between my legs. Maybe you and your father will be mighty glad to have my help one of these days. You won't be carrying such a heavy chip on your shoulder. You remember that, Jamie."

With what dignity he could manage, he vaulted into the saddle and loped away. Honey had been busy at the fire, a few yards off. He came to the wagon now, carrying a dutch oven that had been buried in the coals. Jamie knew he had overheard Arnett's parting threat.

"The conceited ass!" she burst out. "God forbid that we'll ever have to turn to him for help, Honey."

"I agree with you, missy," Honey observed with a sober wagging of his head. "You all might git it, but it would be on his terms."

"That's what I meant, Honey."

Next morning the Arkansas was still running an angry torrent. Brewster moved up with his outfit, with the apparent intention of putting it across. No one else was moving. Along the bank, fifty men were watching. Kinnard and Jesse rode over to have a word with him. Brewster was still looking the situation over.

"You better not try it, Nick," Jesse advised, as a dead tree went bobbing and spinning past them. "You're goin' to git some stuff drowned if you do. The river's droppin'. Why not wait till this evenin' or tomorrow like the rest of us are doin'?"

"Because she may be worse tomorrow than she is right now. She can go up faster than she comes down. We don't know what's happenin' up in the mountains, Jesse. I was here once with a big herd. We held up for a day. The river dropped some. It was still dangerous, so we decided to wait. Next morning the Arkansaw was really wild. We stayed here five days before we could get across. I ain't goin' to make that mistake this time."

He shouted an order that put his cows in the water. They were in trouble almost at once. His horses fared no better. The scourings of mountain valleys, hundreds of miles away, were being swept down-stream at express-train speed. The cattle got tangled up in the debris. A dripping limb drove its jagged nose against a 44 rider and knocked him out of the saddle. He clung to the horn and made it across, half a mile below.

It took Brewster better than two hours to get his outfit across.

"He had his way about it and he took a big

losin'," Jesse said sourly, as he and Kinnard rode back to the wagon. "I saw at least thirty-five head go down, and some hosses. He was lucky to save his wagons."

"I know," Kinnard conceded. "But he proved you can get across. He's been here often enough to know something about the ways of this river. If it keeps on dropping, we'll wait; if it starts rising again, we'll make our move. I don't intend to be stalled here for four or five days."

It was the beginning of an argument that lasted all morning, Kinnard watched the river carefully. It continued to drop until early afternoon. Unmistakably then it began to rise. Over Buckmaster's protests, he ordered the herd moved up.

"We'll have it easier than Brewster did if we go now," he insisted to Jesse.

He spoke to Jamie.

"You put your horse in the water before we push the cows in," he told her. "Don't try to fight the current; let it take your horse down-stream. You can work over to the north bank and climb out without any trouble. I don't want any argument from you, Jamie; I want you to do exactly what I tell you. Don't be afraid."

He had never been so firm with her.

"All right, Frank," she agreed with surprising docility.

Within the hour they were ready to cross. Kinnard held his breath as he saw the current carry her away. But she kept her head and gradually neared the far bank. With a grunt of relief he saw horse and rider climb out on dry land.

The crew got the herd leaders into the water without much difficulty but the cows refused to follow. Only the weight of numbers behind them forced them in. Once they found themselves borne along by the swirling flood, they began swimming, bawling with fear. The horses, the riderless ones, were as panic-stricken as the cows. A direct crossing of the river would have been impossible; by quartering across it and letting the current sweep them toward the opposite bank, they managed it. Not all made it. Kinnard saw a score of cows carried away.

There wasn't so much driftwood coming down now. What there was was heavier. A log stuck its black snout out of the water and seemed to charge at Buckmaster. Kinnard saw it.

"Turn away from the bank, Jesse!" he yelled in time. Even so, the water-soaked log hit the rump of the old man's horse a glancing blow that rolled it over on its side for a dangerous moment. Met head on, it would have killed the animal and very likely have sent Buckmaster to his death.

The wagon was sent across last. Logs had been lashed to the sides of the wagon box for greater buoyancy. There was little Honey could do but hold the reins and pray that the horses would eventually reach the opposite bank. The current swept that way near Bidler's store. Jim Travis and Johnny managed to drop their loops over the floundering team and pull it into shallow water. The entire operation had taken little more than an hour. But the afternoon was gone before the herd had been assembled and the remuda rounded up. Jamie's father did not share the satisfaction that the others felt.

"We got acrost, but look at the price we paid," the old man stormed. "It was only luck we didn't lose more. I warned you, Kinnard, but you was too bullheaded to listen!"

Kinnard was ready for him. "Look at the river now," he invited. "We'd have been stuck over there if we'd waited. Won't be any outfit crossing tomorrow. As for the stock we lost, it belonged to me; it was my cows that went under. All you're out is the horse we lost. You ought to congratulate yourself instead of complaining. We'll camp here tonight and be on our way in the morning."

They reached the single track main-line of the Santa Fe in mid-morning. The trail from Bidler's Station to Abilene had been used so much in the days when the town was the Kansas Pacific railhead that the hooves of uncounted thousands of Texas longhorns had churned the prairie sod to dust. It was impossible to stray from that tawny ribbon without knowing it.

Finding accessible water became the problem

now. On their second night out from Bidler's Station, they had to pay for the privilege of watering the stock in a man-made ranch pond. A long drive the following day brought them to the Smoky Hill. The stream was low, but the water was good, and it was free. That evening they discussed whether to stay with the trail another day or swing north in the morning. There was abundant sign that Nick Brewster had bedded down here the night before.

"I'm for headin' north," Buckmaster argued. "For all we know, that's what Nick's doin' today. If we stick to the trail, chances are we'll have to pay for water again."

"He knows the country, Jesse," said Kinnard. "That's the only reason I suggested tagging after him till we see where he turned off. But I don't suppose it makes any great difference. We can get across in the morning and strike off for the northwest and take our chances on finding water."

"Frank, we can't be too far from Ellsworth," Jamie remarked tentatively.

"No, we ought to be seeing it about evening, day after tomorrow."

"If there's any question about water, why not stick to the Smoky Hill?" Jim Travis inquired. "Wouldn't it take us to Ellsworth?"

Travis seldom had much to say. When he did speak, it was usually worth listening to.

"It would, if we could get through the barbed

wire," Kinnard answered. "Brewster warned me not to try it; he said we'd run into a lot of it if we did. Besides, these Kansas rivers are all over the map getting anywhere. You can't make time following them; they turn back on themselves so often that you have to travel two miles to make one. We'll cross in the morning and forget the Smoky Hill."

Putting the cattle across the shallow stream was accomplished without difficulty. Even so it was seven o'clock before Kinnard got away. The cloudless sky had a brassy look, promising an exceedingly hot day. By mid-morning that promise was being fulfilled. With a dry, parching wind burning his face, he ranged far ahead. He had seldom been unable to return to the outfit at noon, with water for that night located. But not today. Noontime passed and the afternoon wore on as he continued to crisscross the waterless prairie in ever-widening sweeps.

In view of the kind of day it had been, he knew the cattle were suffering already. He did not magnify the seriousness of the situation; he knew the cows could go through the night without water, if that became necessary. On the other hand, experience had taught him that nothing could pull down the vitality of a trail herd as quickly as such an experience. The real effect of it would not be felt for two or three days.

His searching was in vain and for the first time they were forced to dry-camp.

The following day was equally discouraging. With desperation driving him, he ranged further to the east. Late in the afternoon he found faint wagon tracks. After following them for less than a mile he was rewarded by the sight of a squat, ramshackle ranch house. In a hollow some distance from the house the westering sun glinted on the placid surface of a sizeable pond. It was fenced off, and as he passed, he saw a crudely lettered sign that said: "No Trespassing."

Two men stepped out of the house as he pulled up. They were unkempt, shaggy-haired, dressed in butternut jeans and coarse homespun shirts. Kinnard saw at a glance that what he had to deal with were a couple of ignorant, embittered Jayhawkers of the worst type. He took it for granted that they were father and son. The latter, a hulking youngster in his early twenties, carried an old rifle cradled in the crook of his left arm. The rifle bespoke their hostility to strangers.

Kinnard told them how he came to be there and explained his need of water.

"We uns ain't sharin' our water with no one," the father informed him. "It ain't rained in weeks and we ain't lookin' fer it to rain right soon. Thet sign on the fence means what it says, mister. We uns need thet water."

"If that bunch of cows down in the meadow is all you're running, you got water enough to take care of your needs for a year."

The argument fell on deaf ears.

"We uns ain't arguyin' with yuh, stranger. If yuh want to go to the trough and water yore hoss and take a swig yourself, we uns ain't got no objection. But yuh ain't waterin' no herd in our pond."

Kinnard got down and walked his horse to the log trough. The thirsty horse sank his muzzle deep in the water before he started to drink. The example appealed to Kinnard and he washed his face, too. He was far from discouraged. Once before Jesse and he had paid for water. In that instance, they had been told at once that they would have to pay, and how much. He was convinced that what the Jayhawkers wanted was money, and that their refusal to come out and say so was a stratagem to boost the price. When he got back to them, he said:

"We wouldn't expect to help ourselves to your water this evening and again in the morning, before we drive on. Would you consider selling us the privilege?"

The old man nodded.

"We uns would—for cash money, that is."

"How much you asking?"

"Two-bits a head."

"Those are fancy prices," Kinnard laughed,

but with very little amusement. "How much is a longhorn steer worth around here?"

"Fifteen, twenty dollars—"

"That's what I figured. It wouldn't take long for him to drink up what he's worth at two-bits a throw. I'm afraid we can't do business."

Swinging into the saddle, he picked up the reins as though to ride away. By appearing to consider it useless to discuss the matter further he hoped to force the man's hand. He was rewarded at once.

"Yuh don't have to go off in a huff, mister. We uns is willing to dicker a bit. I reckon we could make it ten cents a head."

"Not interested," Kinnard said flatly. "We'll pay you ten dollars. You can take it or we'll find water somewhere else."

"Then yuh want to start lookin', mister!"

"Yo're right, Pappy," the young one growled. "He'll be back when he don't find none."

Jamie had become increasingly worried as the long afternoon passed and Kinnard did not return. She agreed with her father that the likeliest explanation was that for the second day he could not find water. But now, with evening coming on, it no longer satisfied her. Dropping back, she spoke to her father.

"It must be something more than not finding water, Dad," she said without attempting to dissemble her anxiety. "Do you suppose he's in trouble somewhere?"

"No, I don't believe there's any reason to think so. It's this dry country; we ain't seen a trickle of water in two days and chances are he ain't either. Considerin' the kind of a day it's been, he knows these critters have just about got to have water this evenin'. He don't have to hear 'em complainin' to know that. We still got some daylight left, an hour or more. Like as not he'll be showin' up before dark."

"What if he doesn't?"

"We'll stop for the night and go out lookin' for him." He had to raise his voice to make himself heard above the bawling of the cattle. "Don't worry about Kinnard! He can take better care of himself than these dang cows can!"

Jamie went back to the head of the herd. Telling her not to worry brought her no peace of mind. Indeed, it was not until she saw Kinnard riding toward them, half an hour later, that she was able to draw a breath of relief.

"We'll have to hold up a bit and have a talk!" he called to her as he passed.

The herd soon lost its momentum. The condition of the cattle strengthened him in his resolve to give them water, whatever came of it. With the Buckmasters and the crew gathered around him, he explained why he was so late getting back and recounted what had passed between him and the two Jayhawkers.

"Before we go any further, we got to decide what we're going to do," he said. "The stuff is drooping for water. They'll smell it a long way off. If they get a whiff of it we won't be able to hold them back. If we don't cut the wire for them, they'll knock it down. Either way, there'll be hell to pay. I mean gunfire."

"You say there's only two of 'em—the old man and his son." Ike Jarvis spoke up. "We ought to be able to take care of them. You tried to be fair, you offered 'em ten dollars. God knows that's more'n enough."

"It is," Kinnard agreed. "But this is a shakedown, Ike. Other outfits have been in trouble here. Those birds know they've got us where the hair is short. They can get help from somewhere. Otherwise, they wouldn't have a chance against a trail outfit of from eight to twelve men."

"Frank, I know we can't go on without water," said Jamie. "But instead of talking gunfight, can't we reach a compromise?"

"Offer them more money, you mean—fifty dollars, a hundred?" Kinnard shook his head unhesitatingly. "I'd never agree to that."

"Nor me!" Jesse growled. "What kind of human skunks can they be, gougin' money out of a man whose cows are sufferin' for water? I say to hell with 'em! If they want a fight they can have it."

"And most likely tomorrow or the next day

we'll have a Kansas sheriff swooping down on us."

"I'll take my chances with the law," her father asserted grimly. "If we show these Jayhawkers we mean business, they may change their tune . . . How long is it goin' to take us to reach that water, Kinnard?"

"It'll be after dark. The moon will be getting up late tonight. That will help us some; we may be able to slip in and cut that fence before they know what's going on. They'll hear the cows coming. No way of preventing that."

He turned to Jamie, and his manner was determined.

"I want you to stay back at the wagon with Honey while we're watering the stock. You sure you understand that?"

"Yes," she acknowledged grudgingly. "It's all right for the rest of you to expose yourself to danger but I'm to stay back where it's safe."

"That's exactly what it amounts to," he replied, gruff and to the point. "After we've watered, we'll move on three or four miles before we bed down and take our chances on finding water during the morning. If we don't have any luck, it won't be too bad; we'll be outside Ellsworth by nightfall."

Addressing them all, he said:

"It may be nine, ten o'clock before we eat supper tonight. We'll push the stuff along till dark. Two of us will go ahead then and cut the wire." He looked the crew over. "Will you go in with me, Jim?"

In selecting Travis over the others he was expressing the confidence he had come to have in him.

"Okay," Jim Travis nodded, aware of the danger they would be running but not hesitating.

When darkness fell, the bawling, bleary-eyed herd was willing enough to be stopped. They stood around, drooping, heads lowered. There was some grass, but only a few were interested.

Jamie rode up to Kinnard. He and Travis were ready to leave.

"Frank, I'm scared," she said, almost crying. "I shudder when I think what may happen to you. I don't suppose it will do any good to ask you to be careful."

His mouth lost its hardness and for a moment he didn't trust himself to speak.

"This is something that has to be done, Jamie. I don't like it any better than you. But nothing is going to happen to me. I'll be all right if you'll just hold that thought."

"I will, Frank," she whispered, conscious of the quivering of her chin but powerless to prevent it. "I—I promise you I will—"

From the saddle, he leaned down and placed his hand gently against her cheek. He meant it as no more than a comforting touch but the feel of her set his blood to pounding and he drew his hand away quickly.

"Thank you, Jamie," he said huskily.

The early night was darker than it would be later. Kinnard and Travis took advantage of it to reconnoiter the house carefully before they moved down to the pond. A faint light burned within, at the rear. They watched, thinking someone might come out. But they neither saw nor heard anyone.

"We'll risk it now, Jim," Kinnard said under his breath.

They cut the fence, two strands of rusted barbed-wire, and lifted several of the posts out of their loose holes. It didn't take long. They had finished and were moving back to their horses when the night brought to their ears the swift running of ponies approaching the rear of the house.

"Getting reinforcements," said Kinnard. "I figured they would."

"How many would you say, Frank?"

"Not more than two or three."

The newcomers reached the house. There was some talk, too far away to be understood, and the banging of a door as they went inside.

"Looks like they mean business, but they don't seem to expect us to show up for some time,"

Travis observed stolidly. "How do you think they'll play it?"

"There's a log water trough in the yard. If there's as many as four of them, a couple will lay out there. One of them will post himself behind that little knoll we passed, off there to the right. I don't know where we can look for the fourth man. Somewhere on our left, I suppose."

"That's if they don't discover that the fence is down—"

"I don't believe that'll make any difference, Jim. They'll hunt what cover they can and that's the best they've got. We can drive them out if we get up in back of them."

They moved away in the darkness. When they had gone several miles, they pulled up to wait for the herd. Kinnard used the time to settle on what he wanted the crew to do.

"I believe I got it worked out, Jim. I want you to take Johnny and Lin and swing up to the right and chase out whoever is on that little knoll. That shouldn't give you any trouble. When he runs, let him go and the three of you circle up in back of the house. Work around to the front and see what you can do about the trough. I'll go up on the other side with Ike and Steve. We ought to reach the house about the same time you do."

"That makes sense," said Travis. "We'll go in before the herd comes up, of course."

"Yeh. I'm purposely leaving Jesse out of this.

We need someone to push the cows along till they smell water. He can do it. He'll have his hands full for a few minutes. It won't give the rest of us any more time than we need."

Travis, silent and relaxed, rolled a cigarette and smoked it leisurely.

"Frank, do you figure these Jayhawkers will put up much of a fight?"

"No. They'll do a lot of shooting, hoping to bluff us out. They'll kill some cows for us, no question about that; but I don't believe they'll stand up to a real fight. There's no reason why they should. And that goes for us, too. As I said before, if they start running let 'em go. We ain't interested in killing them. Remember that."

They heard the approaching drive some minutes before they caught sight of it. It wasn't so dark now, but the moon would not be up for another hour. They rode out to meet the drive. Kinnard spoke to Buckmaster and the others. As soon as they reached an understanding they left Jesse with the herd and raced to the pond. They were still some distance from it when Kinnard motioned for Travis to head off to the south with Johnny and Lin. He turned off in the other direction with Portugay and Ike.

Kinnard led them away from the house for a few minutes and then swung back toward it. They had a long gentle slope ahead of them. Spreading out, they went up it slowly, walking their horses.

Portugay was on his left, Ike to the right of him.

Searching out the slope's darkness, Kinnard's eyes fastened on a clump of stunted cedars, several hundred yards away. Since it was the only spot that offered concealment, he was confident that if there was a Jayhawker ahead of them, he was there. Risking a low call, he warned Steve and Ike to be wary of the cedars. He kept an ear cocked for sound of the herd. He knew it wouldn't be long now before the thirst-crazed cows would be thundering toward the pond.

Suddenly a gun flashed on the knoll, far to the right. A hornet's nest of angry shots erupted immediately.

Kinnard nodded to himself, understanding the pattern of the shooting. Obviously Travis and his party had found someone and were giving him a bad time. The shooting ended as abruptly as it had begun. He took that as evidence that the bushwhacker had fled.

But the echo of that flurry of gunfire had barely died away when the thunder of the onrushing herd rolled over the prairie in a wild crescendo. Instantly the night became hideous with crack of rifle fire from the water trough. Ahead of him Kinnard caught the red muzzle bursts of a gun in the clump of cedars. At that indefinite target he, Ike and Portugay took aim. Their bucking guns failed to dislodge the unseen sniper. But his shooting was as ineffectual as theirs.

The cattle had reached the pond. The rattle of clashing horns filled the air as they fought one another in their frenzy to get to the water. The wire that had been cut didn't provide opening enough. With lowered heads they charged into the standing fence and brought it down. The first ones to get through were pushed far out into the water by the pressing hundreds behind them. Their own agony wasn't enough; from the direction of the water trough winged messengers of death whined into their midst.

According to Kinnard's calculations, Travis had had time enough to reach the house and be in position to do something about stopping that murderous fire from the trough. He knew it had to be stopped, and quickly. Refusing to be held up any longer by the searching shots from the clump of cedars, he gave Ike and Steve a yell and the three of them charged up the slope, firing as they went.

And now from the house came rattling gunfire. It was angry and brief. A few moments later it was followed by several retreating shots.

"Jim," thought Kinnard. "He's got 'em on the run!"

When they reached the cedars, they found no one there. As they paused, a gun flashed further up the slope.

"He seems to be the only one of them left with any fight in him," said Kinnard. "Spread out again and we'll send him hightailing."

They advanced as they had before, Steve on the left, Ike to the right and Kinnard in the middle. The fight, to all intents, was over and had gone his way. He was eager to learn the cost, but he didn't grow careless in his eagerness. Coming out of a dip at the top of the slope, he caught the flash of a gun, off to his left and slightly ahead, a split second before sound of the shot hit the air. He ducked unconsciously as the screaming slug narrowly missed his head.

He couldn't understand a shot coming from that direction, unless the man they were chasing had doubled back. He didn't have more than a second or two to think about it, when that mysterious gun flashed again. The bullet struck him under the left arm. He felt its red-hot stab in the moment before he lost consciousness and tumbled to the earth.

In the stillness that followed, Ike Jarvis heard Portugay yelling:

"Come quick! Kinnard's down! That bastard dropped him!"

He found the little man bending down over Kinnard.

"Let me have a look at him," Ike growled, pushing him aside.

Portugay's eyes glittered wickedly in the

darkness and there were lines in his face that emphasized its cruelty.

"It's no use," he muttered savagely, "He's dead."

Ike got down on his knees and made a hurried examination.

"No, he ain't!" he declared with a gulp of relief. "He may be dyin', but he ain't dead. You git some of the boys up here in a hurry, Portugay. We'll get Kinnard to the wagon somehow."

10

Travis came in to tell Jamie. He was the strong man of the outfit now. That he came alone warned her that something was wrong.

"I could hear the shooting, Jim. It was terrible." She steeled herself, knowing that the question that trembled on her lips had to be asked. "Is it my father?"

"No, Kinnard. The rest of us didn't get so much as a scratch. We lost some cows, as many as eight. They're moving the stuff this way now. We'll have to bed down here; they've had too much water to move them tonight."

He knew he wasn't telling her what she wanted to know. In the yellow glow of the lantern suspended from the wagon, he could see how drawn and bloodless her face was. By marking time, he hoped to give her a chance to pull herself together.

"Jim—was he killed?"

"No, he's hurt bad. Ike says it was the last shot that got him. They're bringing him here. He needs a doctor, Jamie. We'll have to get him into Ellsworth as quickly as we can. It can't be more than sixteen miles or so. We'll have to rearrange the wagon and make a bed for him."

"Of course. I'll help you—"

"If you will. It'll give Honey a chance to make some coffee and dish up a bite of something."

He spoke to Honey, telling him what he wanted.

"You know the team," he said. "It's going to be up to you to get Kinnard to town. One of us will go with you."

"I'll go," Jamie volunteered at once. "I want to, Jim. The Kansas Pacific runs to Ellsworth. We can't be far from it right now. When we hit the tracks, we'll follow them west till we find a road. We won't lose our way."

"You shouldn't," he agreed. "It'll be nine or half-past before you get started. If you keep the team moving right along, you ought to be in town an hour or so after midnight."

While Honey cooked coffee and set out a cold supper, they rearranged the wagon so that Kinnard might be made as comfortable as possible.

"We're paying a terrible price for a little water," Jamie remarked, as they worked. She had got a grip on herself, but there was a hidden ache in her heart that was almost impossible for her to conceal.

"If Frank pulls out of this it won't be too high," Travis told her. "Just because he hasn't regained consciousness is no reason to think he's going to die. There's been very little bleeding. The slug may have shattered a rib, but if that was the case he'd be in some pain. He doesn't seem to be; he acts like he was paralyzed. It's my opinion that the slug followed the rib around and lodged against the spinal cord. I think that's what has got him stunned. The doctors have a name for it . . . You got any money on you, Jamie?"

"No—"

"Get some from your father. You'll have to stay in town. Send Honey back. We'll meet him somewhere during the morning and be in Ellsworth toward evening."

They were ready and waiting when Kinnard was brought in and lifted into the wagon. To see him lying so still, the pallor of his face showing through the tan, almost overcame Jamie.

She had taken her seat beside Honey and they were about to go, when Ike Jarvis climbed up on the wheel and spoke to her, and to her alone. "When the doc removes the slug, you ask for it, Jamie. Frank will want it."

"For what reason, Ike?" she asked, not understanding.

"As a souvenir," the old puncher lied. "If he don't want it, you git it for me, Jamie. I'd sure like to have it."

Jamie was never to forget that midnight drive into Ellsworth. The team had already put in a long day, but time after time she urged Honey to whip them up.

After crossing the Kansas Pacific tracks, they

found a fairly well-traveled road in another hour that took them into town. It was after one o'clock when they got there. Ellsworth's wild days were over, but it still refused to be put to bed at a reasonable hour. Hailing two men standing on the plank sidewalk in front of the old Ellsworth House, Jamie asked to be directed to a doctor.

"Doc Schramm is the best man in town," she was told. "Second house around the corner."

Peter Schramm, a giant, muscular German, finished eating his usual bedtime snack as he listened to what she had to say.

"I get him in and have a look at him," said he. And when Jamie suggested that he might need help, it produced an amused, guttural laugh. "By golly, he must be big if I can't carry him."

When he had placed Kinnard on the table, he stripped him to the waist and with quick, sure hands examined the wound and searched for the path the bullet had taken. A series of grunts escaped him as his fingers progressed. It was as though he was conducting a debate with himself. Turning his patient over on his stomach, he continued his exploration.

"Yah, here it is!" he exclaimed of a sudden and with the satisfaction of a hunter who had bagged his game. Indicating a spot just removed from Kinnard's spine, he glanced up at Jamie. "There's your bullet—glanced off a rib and ended up here.

By golly, this boy was lucky. Another inch and he would never have walked again."

"You mean he'll live, doctor?" Her throat was so tight that she had to push the words out.

"Live?" he chuckled. "Of course he will—at least till he gets shot again. You go in the sitting room and wait. Probing for a bullet is nothing to watch. I'll call you when I want you."

Jamie breathed a silent prayer as she waited. She cried a bit, and as the tension ran out of her, she felt suddenly weak and exhausted. After what seemed a long time the doctor came in holding up the extracted bullet for her inspection.

"It's an ugly little thing, isn't it?"

"I'd like to have it, doctor—"

"You would?" Schramm sounded surprised. "Well, take it."

Jamie shook her head. "I couldn't bear to touch it. Won't you put it in an envelope for me, please?"

"Yah, I will. I'm going to finish undressing him now and put him to bed. I have a couple rooms I keep for such emergencies as this. I want you to go to the hotel and get some sleep. You look ready to collapse. You come back in the morning, after breakfast."

"Is he conscious, doctor?"

"No. It may be three or four hours before his brain begins to function. His nerves have had terrific shock. But I promise you he's going to be all right."

He walked to the door with her.

"Remember you're to have only a few minutes with him in the morning," said he. "He'll need all the rest and quiet he can get tomorrow."

"Certainly," she murmured. "I want to do whatever is best for him . . . Doctor, can I ask one more question? Will we be able to take him north with us?"

"Yah, after a couple days. But I must warn you, he'll be helpless and weak as a kitten for a week or more."

"We can make a comfortable bed for him in the wagon . . . I'll take good care of him."

Doctor Peter Schramm looked down at her and smiled for the first time.

"I'm sure you will, Miss Buckmaster."

Jamie awakened somewhat refreshed. After hurrying through breakfast she came out of the dining room to walk into Worth Arnett. He explained his lack of surprise at seeing her at once.

"News travels fast in a little town like this," he said. "I heard that you'd brought Kinnard in during the night, badly wounded. How did it happen?"

She had no reason to suspect his real reason in wanting to find out how Kinnard had been shot and by whom.

"We had some trouble about water," she told him, anxious to be on her way.

"Then you don't know who got him?"

"No we don't, Worth. He's going to live; that's all that's important. I've got to ask you to excuse me; I'm on my way to the doctor's house."

"I won't keep you but a minute." He was secretly relieved. "Where is your outfit?"

"They'll be in this evening."

After giving it a moment's consideration, he said:

"We're ready to pull out now. Maybe I better lay over and have a talk with your father."

"For what purpose?" she inquired with a disdainful toss of her head.

"Jamie, you can't go on without Kinnard. I got a good man in Cim Smith who'll get us through. We can throw the two outfits together. I'm willing to make your father the offer."

"That's very generous of you," she replied with cutting sarcasm. "I'm afraid you've been misinformed. We have no intention of going on without Frank."

"That's silly, Jamie, laying over here till he's back on his feet." Arnett acted as if he couldn't believe his ears.

"It may be silly," she retorted as she brushed past him, "but when we leave Ellsworth, Frank will be with us."

There was a worried look in her eyes as she went up the street. She knew that what she had said was a hope rather than a certainty. Not knowing what awaited her, she turned the corner and rang Dr. Schramm's bell. She sensed the moment he admitted her that his news was good.

"He's better, doctor?"

"Yah, yah. I told you he'd be all right. I been talking to him. You go in now; he's expecting you. I give you ten minutes."

A strange sense of embarrassment touched her as the door closed and she stood at the foot of the bed gazing at Kinnard. She didn't try to explain it, but suddenly she didn't want him to know how much this moment meant to her.

"Frank, I—I'm happy to see you so much better," she murmured timorously. "I was terribly afraid you weren't going to make it."

He managed a feeble smile that had a tenderness that was unnerving to her.

"I guess I wouldn't have made it but for you, Jamie. I been talking to the doctor. He told me how you brought me in . . . Can't you find a chair and sit here beside the bed?"

She drew up a chair and sat there trying to appear composed and sure of herself.

"I've got so much to tell you in a few minutes that I don't know where to begin," she said apologetically. "We had some stock killed last night—eight to ten head. Father and the crew are all right. They'll be here this evening."

"I want to see your father, Jamie. He'll have to take on a couple new men. Ellsworth will be the last chance to get them . . . Anything been said about who shot me?"

"No. I don't suppose we'll ever know. Do you think we'll have any trouble with the law, Frank?"

"I doubt it. Those Jayhawkers will dress out those beeves and be well repaid for the damage we did."

She told him about her encounter with Arnett.

"He didn't know what to say when I informed him we were going to lay over here until you could go north with us."

He gazed at her without speaking for a moment or two, a melting light in his eyes. Reaching out slowly, he placed his hand on hers.

"Jamie—was that your idea?"

"Yes—you needn't worry about Father agreeing to it."

"No," he sighed, shaking his head, "you can't afford to wait; time's too precious, Jamie—"

"But the doctor says we can move you day after tomorrow. That'll cost us only one day. We'll make a bed for you in the wagon. I've got it all worked out in my mind. You won't be too uncomfortable."

"That's mighty kind of you," he said with a spare smile. "I appreciate it. But I'll be a nuisance to all of you until I can get back in the saddle."

The doctor rapped on the door when her ten minutes were up.

"I'll be back this evening, Frank."

"Thanks, Jamie," he smiled. "Before you go, tell me why you asked Schramm for the slug he dug out of my back."

"Why, Ike Jarvis told me you might want it. He said he'd like to have it if you didn't. I don't know what he'd want with it."

"I think I do," he nodded. "Keep it for Ike, Jamie."

As the long, hot day began to fade into night, Jamie seated herself on the hotel porch, where she could intercept whoever came in from the wagon. She had spent half an hour before supper with Kinnard and found him definitely on the mend. His voice was stronger and there was a trace of color in his face. She had come away so encouraged that she was eager to talk to her father.

What life there was in Ellsworth always flowed past the hotel in the evening. As she sat there, with only the porch railing between herself and the sidewalk, a red-haired young man limped past, glanced her way, looked again and then stopped. She recognized him at once.

"Rusty Johnson!" she cried. "What are you doing in Ellsworth?"

She had known him both in the Panhandle and Oklahoma. He came to the rail, grinning.

"I came up with a beef outfit this spring that

was bound for North Platte. I been laid up here for a couple months with a broken leg. I'm still limpin' a bit."

"So I noticed."

"How's your pa?"

"Fine. I'm waiting for him right now. I suppose you know the leases were cancelled."

"Yeh, I read about it in the paper. Two or three outfits have gone through here, bound for Montana. I talked to Arnett last night. I never cottoned to him, but I struck him for a job. Got to do somethin'. He said he was full up."

"Rusty, are you fit to ride?" she asked at once, hoping that this chance meeting might prove to be a stroke of good luck.

"I won't say I'm able to work stock just yet, but I can hold up my end with a trail herd."

"Then you've got a job, Rusty. We've got to take on a couple men before we leave here. You see Father tomorrow; we'll be here all day. You've been in town so long you must be well acquainted. Maybe you can help us find a second man."

"I don't know, Jamie," he demurred. "There's no one I'd recommend. You don't want no saddle bum. How does this man Kinnard stack up?"

"You'll like him, Rusty. I suppose you know he was shot."

"Yeh, I'd heard you had to bring him in last night. Who else have you got with you, Jamie?"

"Our old crew and Jim Travis and Steve Portugay."

"Portugay, eh?" He sounded surprised. "Jim's okay; they don't come any better. But Portugay—your pa musta been hard up for a man."

"He was, so many outfits on the move."

"You remember when Arnett had all that trouble with old man Whitmire, a couple years ago, about gittin' the old boy to sell his lease?" Rusty persisted. "The talk then was that Arnett hired little Steve to burn Whitmire out and muss him up."

"No evidence was ever brought forward to prove it, Rusty," she reminded him. "But you don't have to bother about Steve; you do your job and he'll do his."

After he left she couldn't dismiss what he had said from her mind. It had never occurred to her that their misfortunes were related to some mysterious connection between Worth and Portugay. Now that she gave it some thought, it seemed too fantastic for belief. But scoff at it as she might, it left her wondering.

11

She was still considering it when she saw her father and Jim Travis riding up the street. She called to them and they turned into the hotel's hitch-rack.

"I've been expecting you for an hour," she said, as they joined her on the porch. "You better go around the corner to the doctor's right away. Frank wants to talk to you. I told him you'd be in to see him."

"How is he?" Jesse asked.

"He's fine, Dad." She glanced at Travis. "You had the trouble diagnosed correctly, Jim. The bullet was pressing against the spinal cord. Dr. Schramm says we can move him day after tomorrow."

"I don't know about that," Jesse objected. "Who's going to take care of him?"

"I will. It will be for only a week or so. He'll be up and around by the time we reach Nebraska. We need him, Dad," she added earnestly. "We're not going to leave him here in Ellsworth."

"If we can possibly take him, I don't see how we can afford not to," said Travis. "He's getting to country he knows now. We may lose time for a few days, Jesse, but he'll more'n make it up for us by the time we get to Ogalalla."

"That's somethin' to consider, sure enough," Buckmaster conceded. "We've had our troubles but he's got us this far. If he's willin' to risk leavin' before he should, I got no objection. I'll talk to the doctor."

"I hope you do," said Jamie. "I'll sit here until you come back. Has Jim said anything to you about taking on another man or two?"

"Yeh. We'll just about have to do it, with Kinnard laid up. We'll look around tomorrow. I don't know what luck we'll have."

"I've had some already, Dad. I've got one good man for us."

She told them about Rusty Johnson. Her father was as pleased as Travis.

"Rusty's a good man even with half a leg," the latter declared.

"He is," Jesse agreed. "I'll see him in the mornin'."

Left alone, her thoughts turned back to Arnett and Portugay. The seed of suspicion had been planted in her. It grew like a rank weed, compelling her attention.

When her father and Travis returned, they were visibly encouraged.

"He'll make it all right," said Jesse. "That man's got an iron will. I wouldn't have given five cents for his chances last night."

They spoke for some time before she mentioned her meeting with Arnett that morning.

Though she told them what had been said, she was careful to keep her unresolved suspicions to herself.

"He's got more crust than brains, suggestin' that we join up with him," Jesse snorted with unexpected ire. "After tryin' to stampede our hosses and drive us off water we'd found, you wouldn't think he'd have the nerve to make us a proposition like that. He must figger I'm ten kinds of a damn fool."

He seldom expressed himself at such length. As though surprised at his loquacity, he reached hurriedly for his tobacco sack and bit off a chew of his favorite Black Strap.

"He's the kind who, if he can't take you over by pretendin' to do you a favor, will try to do it some other way," he continued, after working his jaws for a minute. "It could be that he's been takin' dead aim on us."

It gave Jamie a start.

"Why do you say that, Dad?"

"It's just a feelin'. Some peculiar things been happenin'."

He refused to say what they were and Jamie could not draw him out. Glancing at his watch, he said:

"It's gittin' late, Jim. We had a hard day. Time to be headin' for camp. We're bedded down about a mile and a half east of town, Jamie. When I come in the morning I'll fetch your hoss.

No reason, though, why you shouldn't stay at the hotel again tomorrow night and git a good rest."

"If I'm going to do that, Dad, I'll ride out and get some clothes. I haven't had a dress on in weeks."

Though it was no later than nine o'clock when she arrived at the doctor's to visit Kinnard, she had been out to the wagon and back and spent half an hour donning her best feminine finery. She found Ike Jarvis with Kinnard. They broke off their conversation so abruptly that she wondered what it was that they didn't want her to hear.

"I was jest goin'," Ike said, getting to his feet and trying to gloss over the awkwardness of the moment. "Frank looks good, don't he?"

"I should," Kinnard spoke up for himself. "I slept like a top and got away with an excellent breakfast." He gave her an admiring glance. "I must say you're looking better than good. You're as pretty as can be."

"I'm not, but I'm obliged to you for saying so," she laughed. "I got tired of masquerading as a man. Seriously, Frank, how are you feeling?"

"Fine. I have some pain, but it doesn't amount to anything. Schramm is going to have a barber come in this morning and give me a shave. Your father and Jim were here about an hour ago. They told me about Rusty Johnson. That's a bit of luck. I hope they can find another good man."

"Rusty didn't seem to think so—"

"So they said. I'll take one good man over two poor ones any time."

She reached in her purse and calling Ike back as he started for the door, handed him the bullet that had felled Kinnard.

"You take it, Ike," she said with a little shiver. "I never want to see it again."

The old puncher left and she took the vacated chair beside the bed. Kinnard's eyes were warm and tender as he gazed at her, so young and lovely this morning. His thoughts were close to the surface and it was with an effort that he stopped short of voicing them. "Some time, perhaps, if things go my way," he told himself. "Not now."

Jamie had come with something on her mind and with her usual forthrightness, she got to it at once.

"Frank, you said some time ago that you didn't trust Steve, that you'd hand him his time if you could find a man to replace him. I presume that's what you intend to do before we leave Ellsworth."

"No, we need him a while longer." His mouth was hard again. "We'll keep him on till I'm back on my feet."

It didn't tell her what she wanted to know. She tried again.

"You never saw Steve Portugay until he caught

on with us," she began with careful indirection. "It seems that he's been mixed up in every bit of trouble we've had. I can't understand it, Frank. He hasn't any reason to hate you."

Kinnard gave her a long, measuring glance.

"What are you driving at, Jamie?"

"At something Father said last night. I guess Rusty first put it in my mind. Dad's known Steve for a couple years or more. We never had trouble with him. I know of no reason why he should want to make things tough for us. See what I mean?"

"I can't say I do," he replied. If he resorted to the lie it was because he thought he knew exactly what she meant and where this was leading them.

"There must be a third party, Frank. That must be the explanation. Worth Arnett hates you; he'd stop at nothing to pull you down. As for our little outfit—if we got into trouble and he thought he could grab it, he wouldn't hesitate a minute."

"Your father said that?" Kinnard asked, his eyes unfathomable.

"He intimated as much. Worth has been playing tag with us ever since we crossed the Salt Fork. He could have been days ahead of us if he had wanted to. There must be a reason."

"Don't you think you're letting your imagination run away with you, Jamie?" he asked, looking away. "Arnett ain't going to take us over."

"That's not my point, and you know it," she said with some asperity. "He could be trying. I'm asking you point blank: do you think Steve's being paid for what he's doing?"

"I haven't given it any thought one way or the other," was his shrewdly evasive answer. "But I will. In the meantime, Jamie, don't say anything about it. It'd be a mistake to go off half-cocked."

It fooled her and she said nothing further about it.

They went on, with Rusty Johnson the only addition to the crew. Steve Portugay regarded him with the congenital suspicion he entertained for all men. Heretofore, he had been in the anomalous position of belonging to the crew but not being accepted as a member by the others. It hadn't mattered to him. But now, as they crossed the Saline and pointed for the South Fork of the Solomon, he seemed to put his habitual sullenness aside and sought to be affable, even with Rusty who bore him an ancient grudge. It had a purpose; he was testing the wind to discover what, if any, danger signals were flying. His overtures met a lukewarm response, which was better than he expected. It fooled him completely. What he didn't know was that everyone in the outfit, save Jamie, was acting under Kinnard's express orders not to show him any antagonism.

Though she was not aware of what was going

on, she sensed that something was afoot. There was a mysterious tension in the air, intangible but there nevertheless. She spoke to Kinnard about it several times but got nowhere. Health was rushing rather than flowing back into his maimed body. With the tilt rolled half-way up on the bows, it was not uncomfortable riding in the wagon under a hot sun. He was sitting up for two or three hours a day by the time they shook off the dust of Kansas and drove into Nebraska.

They were moving right along, doing thirteen to fifteen miles a day. As they neared the Republican, they cut the trails of other outfits that were ahead of them.

"They all seem to be headin' in the same direction," Buckmaster remarked as they sat around the evening fire. Kinnard had joined them for the first time.

"They're pointing for Ogalalla, on the South Platte, Jesse. It's the jumping-off place for Dakota. They'll lay in supplies there and cross the North Platte a little to the west, about old Camp Clark. If they know what they're doing, they'll follow the Sidney-Black Hills stage road and go up Hat Creek and over to the Belle Fourche. That's what we'll be doing. We've got just one bad dry stretch—about thirty miles of it—between here and Ogalalla. There's no way of avoiding it. Of course, it may rain. If it does, there'll be water enough standing in the *charcos* to give us all we'll need."

And then to their surprise, he said that he was going to do some riding the next day.

"You think you should—as soon as this, Frank?" Jamie asked with frank anxiety.

"I'll try not to overdo it. I can't stand being cooped up in the wagon any longer."

He found that a couple hours in the saddle was all he could stand. He tried it again the next day and was out all morning. By the time they crossed the Republican, he was beginning to feel like himself again.

The evening following, they camped at a spring-fed water-hole in a coulee. From the rim, the undulating plains stretched away to the horizon in all directions. All day long, as had become his habit, Honey had been picking up every likely-looking piece of firewood he passed and tossing it into the leather apron suspended below the wagon. It came in handy tonight, for there was not a tree or clump of sage in sight.

Jamie was arranging her blankets for the night, when Kinnard came over to her. The others were lounging in a circle some little distance away.

"Do you mind letting that go for a minute?" he said, his manner unaccountably grim. "I got to talk to you."

She stood up, his tone and the look on his face sending a chill through her. Intuitively she knew that the tension that had hovered over the outfit for days had come to a head.

"Frank, there's been something wrong ever since we left Ellsworth. You're finally ready to tell me what it is—is that it?"

Ignoring her question, he said:

"They may be watching us. I want you to talk quietly . . . I been lying to you about some things ever since you first came to see me at the doctor's. And for two reasons: I wanted to spare you the truth as long as I could, and I was afraid if you knew you might accidentally let something slip that would scare him off."

"By him, you mean—"

"Steve Portugay. When you asked me if I thought Arnett had made a deal with him, I said no. Actually I've thought so ever since the night the attempt was made to run off our horses and Steve warned Arnett away. After the fight with the Jayhawkers there wasn't any room left for doubt."

"Good Lord, Frank, are you telling me Steve tried to kill—"

"I'm telling you we didn't want that slug for a souvenir; we wanted it for evidence. We're going to try him this evening—give him a fair hearing. If he's innocent, he'll get his time; he can gather up his string of broncs and drift. If he's found guilty, we'll string him up on the first tree we come to."

Feeling suddenly weak, she flung out a hand and caught the wheel to steady herself.

"Oh, no, Frank!" she gasped. "You can't do it! You men can't ignore the law and set yourselves up as judge and jury and try a man for his life. He's entitled to justice—"

"He'll get more justice than a paid killer usually gets."

"And my father has agreed to it?"

"Nobody had to talk him into it, Jamie. He knows what the score is." Kinnard's tone was cold and emotionless. "He had Portugay watched night and day while I was lying in the wagon. There's only one question I have to ask you: do you want to sit in or walk out of the coulee till it's over."

Gathering herself up proudly, she said with a low cry of utter contempt:

"You'd prefer me to leave, wouldn't you? It might shame you men to have me present to listen to your ghastly deliberations. Don't mistake what I am saying as sympathy for Portugay. I pity him, but I pity the rest of you more. I don't suppose anything could dissuade you from going through with this ghastly business."

"Nothing," was his wooden, inflexible answer.

"Very well. You go back. I'll follow you over in a minute."

12

When Jamie sat down with the others the circle was complete. Suddenly the talk stilled. Kinnard inclined his head in a little nod. It was the agreed-on signal. Ike Jarvis got up. Stepping around in back of Portugay, he shoved the muzzle of his gun against the little man's head and told him to stand up.

"That's my gun you feel borin' into you," the old puncher informed him. "Stand up and unbuckle your belt."

"What the hell's the idea?" Steve demanded angrily. A horrible suspicion of what it meant flashed across his mind as his eyes swept the circle of hostile faces.

He got up and dropped his belt. There was nothing else he could do. Jim Travis grabbed it and tossed it aside. Ike ordered Steve to get his hands up, and to Johnny Gaines he said:

"Go through him, Johnny, and see if he's got anythin' on him."

Portugay protested violently but he had to submit.

"Don't find anythin'," said Johnny.

"Git his blanket roll, bring it here and open it up," Ike told him.

It had been rehearsed; they were doing as they

had planned. The blanket roll was opened and searched. In a small leather sack Johnny found a little more than three hundred dollars in bills.

It was what they were looking for. It confirmed what they had been thinking and a grunting anger rumbled out of them.

"That's my money!" Steve raged. "Git your goddamn hands off it!"

No one bothered to answer him. Johnny took the money over to Buckmaster and tossed it in his lap. And now Jesse spoke for the first time.

"You can sit down, Steve; this may take a while."

"I don't know what you're gittin' at, but I'll set down, Jesse, and when you're done, you can hand me my time; I'm through with this outfit!"

"We'll git back to the money later," said Jesse Buckmaster, ignoring the little man's outburst again. "I reckon you know what this is all about, but jest so there won't be no doubt about it, I'll tell you," he continued. "This is a court, Steve—not accordin' to law but its findin's will be jest as bindin'. You're on trial for sellin' us out to Arnett and bein' a lying, double-crossin', murderin' skunk. The boys has asked me to act as judge. I'll hear the evidence against you and give you a chance to prove it ain't so before we reach a verdict."

Jamie tried to stop him, but he silenced her sharply.

"Be still or leave," he warned. "I ain't goin' to argue with you."

She could only gaze at her father in sheer amazement, so marked was the sudden change in him. For weeks he had appeared to be a submerged, beaten man, bogged down by the loss he had suffered with the cancelling of the leases. As much as she wanted him to get a grip on himself, she shuddered to think that it had to be born of such a ghastly business as this.

He began to ask questions, going around the circle clockwise, pertaining to those first days on the trail, when Portugay was riding drag by himself and the stragglers had been permitted to string out for miles, adding up to hours and days lost. When he mentioned what had happened north of the Salt Fork, it was their unanimous opinion that Portugay had invented the story about the runaway broncs to enable him to hold a secret rendezvous with Arnett. They hadn't given it much thought at the time, and though they still had no evidence to support their contention, things had happened since then that had given their thinking an ugly slant. It was the same when the talk progressed to the near-clash with Arnett at the mudhole and the bungled attempt to stampede their horses, later that night.

"It seems to be your idea, Kinnard, that it was somethin' he cooked up with Arnett when he saw him on the Salt Fork," said Buckmaster.

"There's no doubt about it in my mind, Jesse. He expected to be standing guard by himself. When I showed up, it scrambled his plans. He had to warn Arnett. That's why he started shooting before they got close."

To a man, they agreed with him. They were coming to the night the whip had been used on Portugay. Jamie's blood began to run cold, knowing they would not spare her feelings. She knew they had made up their mind to hang Steve Portugay. They could have said so then, but they preferred to continue the farce.

Her father mentioned the whipping. To her surprise, Kinnard said:

"We can skip that. No need to go any further into it."

No word escaped Jamie, but she silently thanked him for his consideration. He was speaking about the fight with the Jayhawkers now, recalling how he was moving up the slope with Portugay on his left and Ike on his right. He turned to the latter.

"I'm going to ask you some questions, Ike. What was the situation, there at the last?"

"Why, this fella was up the slope a couple hundred yards and tryin' to git away. I figgered he was shootin' jest to keep us from closin' in."

"You're sure he was up the slope, ahead of us?"

"He sure was! I heard those last two shots. I knew they had to come from your gun or

Portugay's, they was so far to the left of me."

"Was this fellow up the slope using a rifle, Ike?"

"Yeh, and a big one. Sounded like a cannon when he squeezed the trigger. I figger it was one of them heavy old .56-50 Spencers."

Kinnard glanced at Buckmaster and told him to carry on. The latter held up the slug that had been removed from the other's back.

"I'm goin' to pass this around," he said. "I want you to take a good look at it."

It was passed from man to man and back to him.

"Is it a rifle slug?" he asked.

They were agreed that it was not.

"It's too light," said Jim Travis, saying what all knew. "It ain't even a .45 or a .44 slug. It was fired from a light calibre pistol."

"Wal, you got Portugay's gun there," Jesse rapped. "Take a look at it. Tell us what it is."

"It's a Navy .36."

Buckmaster looked them over with a cold, glittering eye and gave the damaging evidence time to sink in.

"Wal, I reckon that's about all we need to know," he announced stolidly. "Portugay, you got anythin' to say for yourself?"

Little Steve's cruel face was pasty with terror. He knew he stood condemned; that nothing he might say could save him. His lips began to move and finally he said, with something that passed for courage with him:

"Git this over with! Don't drag it out!"

"We won't be much longer," Buckmaster advised him. "There's this money—where did you git it, Steve?"

"I had it—"

"No, you didn't," the old man contradicted. "If you'd had three hundred dollars in your jeans, you wouldn't have signed up with me; you'd have headed for Texas. You got this money from Arnett. Why don't you tell the truth? You got nothin' to lose."

"To hell with you, you old mossback!" Portugay snarled. "I ain't tellin' you a damn thing!"

Jesse did not press the question. He picked up the bills.

"As money, there's nothin' wrong with the stuff," he remarked solemnly. "It'll make up for the losses we've had." He placed it in his worn purse. He glared owlishly at Kinnard and the crew. "I reckon you boys have had time to make up your minds. What is he—innocent or guilty?"

"Guilty—guilty on every count!" Ike Jarvis was first to answer. The others agreed with him. Around the circle there was not one dissenting voice.

Jamie got up and walked away. She felt nauseated. When she reached the lip of the coulee, she went on, wanting to get away from the sound of their voices and vengeance-stained faces.

Her presence had restrained them. Now that they were relieved of it, they marched the condemned man over to the wagon and bound his hands together behind his back. They tied his legs together then, at the knees and ankles. As a further guarantee that he would be there in the morning, they tied still another rope around his waist and ran it through the iron eye at the end of the wagon tongue, giving it slack enough to enable him to lie on the ground and sleep, if he could find enough peace of mind to indulge in anything so pleasant.

Jamie saw him lying there when she returned. Speaking to no one, she pulled off her boots and without undressing further, got into her blankets. She lay there for hours, without any thought of sleep. She could hear Portugay stirring and moaning to himself, a few feet away. She understood why they had tied him to the wagon. In that treeless sea of grass there was nothing else to which he could be secured.

Before Johnny Gaines and Rusty went out to ride the midnight watch, they came over and had a look at the prisoner. When old Ike and Lin, whom they were relieving, came in, they too came over for the same purpose. She heard them come and go.

"If he could get away without waking up the

camp, he'd have a start of an hour and a half or better before he was missed."

The thought was still with her when Kinnard and Jim Travis went out to ride the dog watch, from two until daylight.

A surprise awaited them when they jogged back to the wagon in the gray dawn. Portugay was gone, and so was one of his horses. The ropes that bound him had been cut. Kinnard's cry aroused the camp. The effort he made to control his wrath did him credit, but it was too much to ask.

"Who did this?" he raged, as Jesse and the others stared bug-eyed at the slashed ropes.

"I did," said Jamie. "He's been gone more than an hour—"

"You—!"

Into that single word he poured all of his sense of blinding fury and outrage. He raised his hands as though he was about to shake the life out of her. "What are you," he cried, "just a meddling damned fool, or was there something between you and that little rat?"

The ugly suggestion stunned her, but she stood up to him, unafraid.

"I know how angry you are. That's no excuse for such talk. It shames you rather than me. I helped him to escape because I didn't want Dad and you to have it on your conscience that you had hanged him. You'd have regretted it the rest of your life. You could have shot him—he deserved it. That wasn't good enough for you; you had to drag it out, with your mock trial, so you could gloat over his agony."

"That's enough!" he stormed. "You'll regret what you did. Portugay's no mixed-up kid; he's a vicious, hardened blackleg. Don't think we've heard the last of him."

"You're right," Buckmaster growled in agreement. "He'll live jest to git even with us. He'll join up with Arnett, no doubt, but all the time he'll be waitin' to knock some of us off."

He hung his head in bitter anguish and refused to listen to her appeal for understanding.

"I figgered I'd brung you up to be a man, not a snivelin', soft-headed female. But it's over and done with and talk won't change it. We'll pay for it someday. As long as that little rat lives, not one of us is safe; not even you."

As they went on, Jamie found her position next to impossible. Honey appeared to be the only friend she had left in the outfit. Having a racial horror of lynching, he had no fault to find with what she had done. It distressed him to see her so miserable.

"You jest keep yore head up, missy," he told her. "You did right, and they'll come to see it when the hate runs out of 'em."

The night before they reached the dry stretch, it

came on to rain, with some lightning and thunder. The herd had bedded down, but they failed to expel the air from their lungs with that satisfied whooshing sound that a cow will make when it's down and means to stay down.

The wind began to kick up and the storm grew in intensity. Jim Travis rode up to Kinnard and Buckmaster.

"The stuff is getting spooky," he told them. "It won't take much more of this to get them up."

"We may be in for some trouble," Kinnard conceded. "I'll order all hands out."

Jamie went out with the others. The night was pitch black between the flashes of lightning. The men were moving around the herd with their monotonous singing. She had seen that continuous chanting quiet a nervous herd. She recognized Kinnard's voice. Minutes later, he appeared out of the surrounding blackness of the night.

"If they start running, they'll go with the wind," he said. "You move over around to the right and watch yourself."

It was the first time he had spoken to her in two days.

"You think they're going to get up?" she asked.

"If one does, they all will. The air's rank with the smell of burnt-out lightning. They don't like it. The least little thing will set 'em off. You turn around and move off to the right as I told you."

As she swung her horse, the wind got under her

slicker. It slapped with a pistol-like report. That did it. A steer heaved to its feet. In a matter of seconds a thousand were up and running.

"Don't try to stop 'em!" he cried. "Get yourself in the clear!"

She tried, only to have her horse put his foot in a prairie dog hole and stumble. Kinnard caught her as she started to go down. The animal righted himself. With Kinnard racing along beside her, they swung away from the avalanche of thundering hoofs and crashing horns bearing down on them.

Suddenly he was gone and she saw no more of him until they met in the soggy dawn. She knew he had saved her life. She had no time to think of that. Jim Travis and her father flashed past her and she followed them.

Through rain and mud, up and down unseen cutbanks and broken ground, the crew raced on in the inky blackness. It was midnight before they got ahead of the stampeding herd, turned the leaders and got it to milling. When morning came, they were ten miles from the wagon. Kinnard counted noses.

"We're lucky," he said. "Didn't lose anyone."

The storm had passed. The exhausted cattle quieted down. Before long they were looking for grass.

"You go to the wagon and gather up our gear," Kinnard told Jamie. "Tell Honey to hitch up and start rolling this way. I'll send Rusty with you, to help you round up the horses."

He would have turned away. She stopped him.

"Frank, as little as I like being indebted to you, I have to thank you for saving my life last night."

"That ain't necessary," he replied without any sign of unbending. "I was just fortunate enough to be there when your horse started to go down."

She could have slapped his face for setting her down in that fashion.

"I'll make you crawl to me one of these days!" she promised herself as she loped away, her cheeks burning with indignation.

They didn't have to worry about water. It stood in puddles and filled the dips and old buffalo wallows. It made for slow, hard going, and when they crossed the South Platte and bedded down outside Ogalalla, Kinnard was the first to agree with Jesse that the stock was so worn that they would have to lay over for a day or two.

Back in the days before the Kansas Pacific and the Santa Fe had pushed their rails westward through Kansas, and the Union Pacific was the only east-west railroad, Ogalalla had been a great trading and shipping point. Thousands of Texas longhorns had changed hands there, their new owners driving them on to Wyoming and Montana, or shipping them east to North Platte and Omaha. It was no longer the bustling cow-town it had been; when the big herds failed to arrive from the south, it had slipped back into a sad and romantic semi-obscurity, relieved at intervals, as it was now, by the migration of the herds from the Indian Lands of Oklahoma. But it was still, as Kinnard had said, the jumping-off place for the north, where a man could buy supplies and get the news.

At the fire that evening, Jamie made a list of the things Honey needed and gave it to her father. He looked it over carefully.

"That's a lot of flour you're askin' for, Honey," he observed.

"Not too much, Jesse," Kinnard spoke up. "It'll have to get us all the way to Miles City. There's a couple other items that may look top-heavy to you. Honey asked my advice and I figured things out as best I could."

"All right. I'll go into Ogalalla in the mornin'. Honey can drive in as soon as breakfast is out of the way. We'll stow the stuff as we carry it out to the wagon. You boys will want to go in tomorrow. You can do that when I git back."

He was gone most of the morning. He returned with news that seven outfits, Arnett's among them, had preceded them up the trail. He didn't like it.

"I didn't figger there was as many as that ahead of us," he said to Kinnard. "By the time we show up, it's goin' to be a scramble to find range."

"I don't know about that, Jesse. But we don't

want to drop any further back. I spent the morning looking the stuff over. It's the old story; we got some cows that'll have to be destroyed."

"How many?"

"There's seven that are in no condition to go any further. And we got three calves this morning. They'll have to go, too."

Though it gave Jesse Buckmaster a wrench every time worn-out stock had to be killed, he had long since come to realize the folly of doing otherwise.

"Cut the stuff out and git rid of it," he said. "We still got a long ways to go. God knows the important thing is to git there."

Jamie had not been a party to their conversation, but she had overheard it. Ignoring Kinnard, she said:

"It shouldn't be necessary to shoot them. I'm sure I can find someone in Ogalalla who'd be glad to have them. Do you mind if I try?"

"Go in this afternoon, if you like," he told her. "If you can git somebody out here to take the stuff off our hands, it'll be all right with me."

Kinnard's eyes followed her as she walked away.

"I admire her spunk," he muttered. "She's sure got a ramrod up her back."

"I reckon both of you have," Jesse grunted.

When Jamie got down at the hitch-rack in front of Butterworth's General Store, she had to step carefully to avoid the puddles that still pocked Ogalalla's main street. The town was very quiet and Simon Butterworth's half-filled shelves told their own story. She made some trifling purchases before she mentioned her real errand.

"Sam Hustis, our marshal, is the man for you to talk to," Butterworth told her. "By now, he must have forty to fifty head he's picked up for nothin'. It gives his boys somethin' to do, lookin' after 'em."

She found the marshal down the street, drowsing at his desk in his combination office and jail. He shook himself awake.

"Sure, I'd like to have them," he chuckled, when she told him why she was there. "It's gittin' to be sort of a business with me. I've had a lot of stuff given me in the past two or three weeks. It's a purty ragged lookin' bunch, I got. But my boys have got the cows on good grass. They'll flesh up before snow flies. Findin' milk for the calves takes some doin'. The boys ain't lost none yet. You want me to send them out yet this afternoon?"

"If you could," said Jamie. "We'll have them cut out for you."

She had been conscious of a "wanted" notice (or flyer) tacked up on the side wall of the shabby office, as they talked. It began to demand her attention. Turning in her chair for a better look, she felt her heart skip a beat as she found herself staring at a pictured likeness of Kinnard. "Wanted for murder, Frank J. Kinnard," she read. "Reward for information leading to the apprehension of this man. Communicate with Timothy Grady, Sheriff, Deadwood."

"What's the matter, miss?" the marshal inquired as she recoiled, her eyes threatening to pop out of their sockets. "You musta seen one of them before."

"No," she whispered, shaking her head, her throat so tight her voice seemed to die there.

13

With a supreme effort Jamie pulled herself together.

"Those are terrible words, Mr. Hustis—'Wanted for murder.'"

"You git used to it in my job," the marshal laughed. "I've picked dozens of flyers like that out of the mail in my time; I been ramroddin' this town for years. In the old days, when Ogalalla was goin' strong, we used to git the backwash from Deadwood and Miles City. That notice musta been about the last one Tim Grady sent out. It's been up there for ten months or more; I jest been too lazy to tear it up. There'll never be a better time for doin' it than now."

A short, heavy-set man, with the fat of easy living piling up on him, he got to his feet with a grunt and ripped the flyer off the wall.

"Mr. Hustis, if you don't want it, could I have it?" she asked, as he was about to crumple it into a ball and toss it under his desk. "I—I'd like to take it out to camp."

"Sure," he grinned. "Don't try to scare anybody with it who knows anythin' about Deadwood and what happened to Tim Grady."

"Why do you say that?" she queried, not understanding at all.

"Grady was another Plummer. He got himself elected by the underworld riff-raff. As soon as he got the badge, he organized his own gang of thieves and killers and ran Deadwood to suit himself for a year or more. The vigilantes dug him out of his bed one night and rounded up his gang. One got away, they say, but Grady and the rest was left decorating the lamp posts between the Bella Union and Tex Rankin's saloon. After that folks kinda lost interest in the warrants Grady had out."

"But a man was murdered, Mr. Hustis—"

"No question about that. I don't know what the circumstances was. I ain't seen Kinnard in a couple of years."

"Then you knew him?"

"Yeh, he used to come down from the north to buy cattle."

Jamie was anxious to leave. She thought she understood why Kinnard had not come into town with her father that morning. She folded the notice and shoved it into her pocket.

A boy, a lad of fifteen or so, came in. "This is my son Otie," the marshal informed her. To the lad, he said: "Got some more stock for you and Clem—seven cows and three young calves. Miss Buckmaster wants you boys to come out this afternoon and pick 'em up. You find Clem and git out there about five o'clock."

As soon as she was beyond the edge of town,

Jamie lifted her horse to a gallop. She was at the wagon fifteen minutes later. It had not given her time to order her thinking, but out of the quagmire of her confusion, one overriding thought took command of her: Kinnard was in danger and she had to warn him. She had promised herself that she would humble him. That and the other resolves she had made were suddenly so petty they were meaningless.

Kinnard was not in sight. From Honey she learned that he had gone down the river with a fowling piece to shoot some prairie chicken for supper. She took off after him at once. In the course of a mile, she saw him moving along the edge of the willows and high buckbrush that here marked the course of the South Platte. He heard her call and waited for her to join him. Her excitement was communicated to him at once.

"What's happened?" he asked, and with more consideration than he had shown her since the night she had enabled Steve Portugay to get away.

"Frank, I had a terrible experience in town. I've got to talk to you."

She got down, and he led her horse into the shade. Before she had a chance to speak, he said:

"I don't know what you're going to tell me. Before you go any further, there's a couple things I want to say. I'm just as sure as I ever was that it was a mistake to let Portugay go. But that wasn't any excuse for the insulting remarks I made. I don't expect you to forgive me; I just want you to know I'm sorry. I been acting like a pig-headed fool."

At any other time it would have soothed her outraged pride. Coming now, it made what she had to say more urgent and meaningful to her.

"Let's say no more about it, Frank; there's no reason for both of us to be pig-headed . . . Tell me, do you know Sam Hustis, the marshal of Ogalalla?"

"Yeh," he nodded. "I remember him."

"Is that why you didn't go in with Dad this morning?"

"Whatever gave you that idea?" he asked with what she had to believe was honest surprise.

She told him she had been directed to the marshal's office and what had been said regarding the unwanted cows and calves.

"He's sending his two boys out to get them," she hurried on. "They'll be out about five o'clock. You can't risk letting them see you, Frank."

"Why not?" He was more puzzled than ever.

"Because all the while I was talking to Mr. Hustis, out of the corner of my eye I could see a 'Wanted' notice pinned on the wall opposite the one I was facing. I finally had to turn and have a good look at it. This is what I saw."

She pulled out the folded flyer and handed it

to him. He spread it out and gazed at it with an expressionless face.

"So this is what's got you so worked up."

He tore the paper to bits and tossed them away.

"What did you have to say about me?"

"Nothing, Frank. I was afraid to. I let him do the talking."

She repeated what Hustis had told her about Sheriff Tim Grady and his gang.

"That's about right," Kinnard nodded. "One of Grady's thugs got away. It took me some time to catch up with him . . . Jamie, you ought to be able to put two and two together. You remember what happened on the dance floor that night in Canadian Crossing—"

"You mean he was the man?"

"Yeh—"

"What was his name?"

"Hank Fordice. He killed the man Grady accused me of murdering. I wanted to bring him back to Deadwood. Arnett's fool play made that impossible. I was in Miles City when friends of mine in Deadwood let me know that the charge against me had been dropped. That was months ago. Do you think I'd have been fool enough to come north if it hadn't?"

"No—" A load had been lifted from her mind, but it left her feeling exhausted and unsure of herself. "How did you ever get involved in such a mess, Frank? Or shouldn't I ask?"

"There's no reason why you shouldn't know." He motioned for her to sit down. Seated beside her, he spoke freely of his past, something she had never been able to get him to do before. He had been a wolfer, a cowboy and stock buyer.

"I did some gambling, too," he continued. "I was well known in Deadwood; I could always get a poker table in Rankin's place."

"A professional gambler?" she murmured, recalling the thought that had crossed her mind when she first noticed how smooth and untanned his hands were.

"I suppose you might call it that. It made a living for me between times. Grady hated me; he knew I was wise to his set-up. One night a man named Luke Storey lost all he had at my table—a thousand dollars or so. After he left, he did a lot of talking about my game being crooked. It got all over town. That's the worst thing you can say about a gambler. Grady was sure I'd do something about it. According to evidence that turned up later, he had Fordice follow Storey home and kill him on his doorstep. Grady promptly accused me of the murder and got out a warrant. I knew I had to get out of Dakota in a hurry. I went down to Miles City and stayed there till the case against me blew up. Believe me, Jamie, there's no reason for me to hide. If it'll make you feel better, I'll go into town this evening and have a talk with Sam Hustis."

She shook her head.

"That won't be necessary, Frank. I believe you." She gave him a wan smile. "I was so scared."

"It was my fault. I should have told you long ago. Maybe some good will come of it. Maybe we can pull together a little better now."

"I hope so," she murmured, a little catch in her voice. "I've been pretty miserable the past week—"

"So have I, Jamie."

Ten days out of Ogalalla, they left the Black Hills stage road and turned west and then up Hat Creek. They were traveling so fast now that no outfit had overhauled them since crossing the North Platte. Kinnard's knowledge of the country was paying off. The confidence he exuded seeped onto the others. There was a better feeling in camp than there had been. The change in Jesse Buckmaster was most noticeable of all. He no longer doubted that they would make it through to Montana. He knew the stock was not in any condition to face an early, hard, northern winter.

"There's no reason to think that's what we're goin' to git," he told Jamie. "It could hold off and not be too tough. If we can put the stuff on good grass for eight to nine weeks, we'll bring most of it through."

Kinnard had seen fit to acquaint him with

the trouble he had had in Deadwood. It had strengthened Jesse's respect for him.

After going up Hat Creek for two days, they left the bluffs and broken buttes and drove for the Belle Fourche. A week later they were moving down the Little Powder into Montana. They were in cattle country now but they saw no cattle. The explanation was apparent; the grass had been grazed down to the roots.

"We got to git away from this, Kinnard," Jesse declared on their third evening on the Little Powder. The herd had been watered and left to find what grass it could. All hands were washed up, waiting for Honey to call them to supper. "Our stuff's had mighty slim pickin's for three days now. What do you make of it? It can't be the outfits ahead of us who've eaten out the range like this."

"They haven't helped it any, Jesse. But that's only part of the story. Stockmen along the Little Powder use it for spring range and move north toward the Missouri as the season advances. If spring is late, they sometimes hold their stuff here until late in June. Ordinarily getting off the grass then will give it time to come back by early fall. You can be sure that's what they're counting on. They'll be back by the middle of September."

"This grass won't come back this year. The ground's bone dry."

"That depends on how soon the fall rains

come and how long they last. They've had a hot, dry summer through here; there's signs of it everywhere. We'll get away from the Little Powder in another three days and cross over to the Tongue. It's what we find beyond the Tongue and the Yellowstone that we got to worry about."

They were eating supper when they saw an old man, mounted on a white horse, coming up the river. He had a string of three pack animals in tow. There was immediate speculation as to who he might be. Even at a distance Kinnard found something familiar about the bearded old man, with his long hair and his gaunt, lanky frame.

Paying them no attention, the stranger came on. He flung up a hand in a friendly salute as he passed, at a distance of no more than fifty yards. By now Kinnard was sure of his man.

"Stony, you turn in here and light a bit," he shouted.

The old man pulled his ancient white horse to a stop and gave the group around the fire a piercing squint.

"Who is that speakin'?" he called back in a voice that was thin with age.

"Frank Kinnard. I ain't letting you go no further tonight. I want to talk to you. We got meat and biscuits and a potful of coffee. You let old Bess and your pack horses stand awhile, we'll give you a hand with the packs a bit later."

With an agility that belied his years, Stony

Thompson got down from the saddle and strode up to the fire, his back as straight as an Indian's. Kinnard and he were friends of long-standing. Though this was their first meeting in almost two years, he restricted his greeting to a glance from under his hooded brows.

"By grab, yuh look as sassy as ever, son," he cackled.

"And you, Stony? How are you making it?"

"Oh, poor, poor. I'm gittin' too old to git out of my own way. I'm down to poisonin' wolves for the bounty money. Makin' a livin' and thet's about all."

Kinnard introduced him around and explained his connection with the outfit.

"Stony knew this country when it was black with buffalo and swarming with Sioux," Kinnard told Jesse and the others. "The two of us spent a winter together, wolfing up on Milk River. That was back in '79, wasn't it, Stony?"

"Jest about. The pelts was worth sunthin' in them days."

He was dirty and he gave off a ripe odor compounded of sweat, grease and wood smoke. There was nothing wrong with his appetite and he ate with a noisy relish. Eating was a serious business with him, not to be interrupted with idle conversation. When he was finished, he wiped his whiskers with the back of his hand and got out pipe and tobacco. He was ready to talk.

"I'm goin' up to the headwaters of the Little Powder and set out some baits. It'll take me a couple months to work back down here." His attention focused on Jamie. "I been seein' a number of Texas outfits movin' in, but by dad yore the fust female I seen. Yuh mean to tell me yuh come up the trail all the way from Texas?"

"From Oklahoma."

"Wal, that's about the same thing. I don't know what yore pappy and Kinnard expect to find between here and the Missoury. I can tell 'em it ain't goin' to be good. Ain't no grass left in the Bad Lands; country's all burnt out. Ain't a drop of rain fell in three months."

They were hanging on his words now. What he was saying spelled calamity.

"How much moving around have you been doing the past few months?" Kinnard asked, thinking the old man might be exaggerating. Stony sensed the intent of the question.

"Wal, I ain't been sittin' still, son," he answered sharply. "I know what I'm talkin' about. I seen most of it. Thar's a lot of range in eastern Montana, but it's gittin' overstocked. The new outfits thet are comin' in ain't goin' to be welcome, I tell yuh; thar ain't grass enough for them that's been here for years. I tried to talk to one of these newcomers. He never seen the country before but he knew more about it than I do. Yuh can't tell a Texan nuthin'—leastwise most of 'em," he added, remembering where he was.

"You know his name, Stony?"

"Naw. A big tall fellar—"

"How was his stuff branded?"

"A in a box—"

"That's Arnett's brand—Box A," Jim Travis said at once. There was a nodding of heads.

"So yo're acquainted with the gent?" Stony's tone was disparaging.

"We are," said Kinnard. "You got any idea where he's making for?"

"I don't figger he knows himself. Goin' into Miles City, of course . . . Where you headin', son?"

"Why, I was going to cross the Yellowstone at Fort Keogh and see what we could find in that nest of creeks to the west of Smoke Butte. What you say has me sort of scared out."

"I hope so, son. Don't yuh try that country; them cricks has all gone dry and the grass is as brown as a bear's ass." Belatedly remembering that he was in mixed company, he apologized for his language. "When yuh git acrost the Yellowstone, strike straight for the Musselshell. It's fordable any place right now. Yo're acquainted with that country. When yuh hit Flat Willow, go up the crick. Thar's cattle in thar; Con Gerstenberg's got a big herd and so has Kohrs. Yuh allus hit it off good with Con. Yuh got a small outfit; yuh can crowd in. Yuh'll have water and purty good grass. The snow don't lie long on the ground."

"As I remember it," said Kinnard, "there's very little sage in there to hold the snow."

"Thet's right, son. You head for Flat Willow and you'll thank me. Yuh can't beat it in summer, and it ain't bad winter range, with them limestone cutbanks to give stock some perfection."

Jesse Buckmaster had been drinking in every word, and with unconcealed enthusiasm.

"It sure sounds like what we're lookin' for, Stony. We'll have to build cabins. Is there any timber?"

"No hardwood, but plenty yellow pine, cedar and box elder."

The three of them sat by the fire talking long after Travis and Johnny had gone out to stand guard and the others had sought their blankets. Going as far as Flat Willow meant an additional eighty to a hundred miles. The promise it held made it more than worthwhile.

Stony left them in the morning, after breakfast.

"It's sad to see him going off alone like that, so old," Jamie said to Kinnard.

"You couldn't pay him to live any other way. Running into him was a good break for us. The first real piece of luck we've had."

"You're sure you and Dad can rely on what he told you? Don't misunderstand me, Frank. You know what it means to us."

"Since I've known him, he's never lied to me." His tone carried a mild rebuke. "We got to point for Miles City, in any case. That'll give us five to six days to think things over and decide what we want to do."

She had thought it strange that Stony had not mentioned the trouble Kinnard had had in Deadwood. It wasn't merely idle curiosity that led her to mention it.

"He must have known, Frank."

"Certainly. Things like that get a wide circulation." With a smile, he added, "He wasn't sparing my feelings. I got no cloud hanging over me, Jamie. Don't trouble yourself about it."

As they continued down the Little Powder, there was talk about Arnett. They took it for granted that he had Steve Portugay with him.

"I hope we catch up with that pair in Miles City," Ike Jarvis remarked darkly. "There'll be some trouble if we do."

"I don't expect to find Arnett there," said Kinnard. "He'll be in as big a sweat as we are to find some range."

What they were to do when they had crossed the Yellowstone became a far more engrossing topic around the evening fire than settling their grudge against Arnett and Portugay. It was a mistake, as they were shortly to discover.

Surrounding range conditions did not improve as they progressed. The little side creeks were either dry or if they held any water at all, it lay stagnant in separated pools. It drove home the conviction that old Stony knew what he was talking about. Flat Willow began to loom as the promised land.

Through a broken country of bluffs and ragged cliffs, they crossed from the Little Powder to the Tongue, the crookedest river in Montana, in two days. They were less than twenty-five miles from Miles City, the cattle capital of eastern Montana. The Tongue was running low and muddy, a further argument in favor of Flat Willow.

Kinnard's original understanding with Buckmaster was that when they reached Miles City they were to settle their accounts and part company. Though no formal agreement to the contrary had been made, both parties had come to take it more or less for granted that they would go on together. Jesse brought up the matter that evening.

"Conditions being what they are, we better stick together till spring," Kinnard said without hesitation. "We won't know where we stand till then. Is that agreeable to you?"

"It sure is. This is your country; I'd hate to part company with you till I git my feet on the ground. Are we set on Flat Willow?"

"Unless we hear something in Miles City to make us change our minds. The two of us will go in together, Jesse. We'll have to be careful to say nothing about our plans. It'd be too damn bad if we got to Flat Willow and found some other outfit had edged in ahead of us."

The wind that had been blowing all day, shifting from the north to the northwest and back again, had died down at sunset. With the coming of night, it began to kick up again, and as they sat around the fire, it sent sparks flying several times.

"That could be dangerous, sparks flyin' that way," Jesse remarked. "We got miles of dead grass on every side of us. It'd take jest a spark to touch it off."

"You're right," Kinnard agreed. "We'll douse the fire. It's time to turn in anyway."

Lin got up with him and getting a couple of buckets at the wagon, they went to the river, a matter of a few yards, and filled them.

"I guess that does it," Lin observed, as they emptied the buckets on the fire. "Or do you want to make another trip?"

"No, it's out," Kinnard said. The others were in their blankets already. He gazed at the clouds scudding across the moon. "Looks like it's going to blow all night."

"This fringe of scrub timber along the river will be good enough for a windbreak, Frank. We'll be all right here."

Kinnard had no reason to think otherwise. He had been asleep most of the night when he was pulled awake by the sound of the herd heaving to its feet. For a moment, he didn't know what it meant; the night was clear and save for the rushing of the wind, seemingly peaceful. Before he could pull on his boots, Jim Travis, who had been out night-guarding, came pounding in and aroused the camp with the news that the grass was afire to the east and west of them.

"The stuff's going to run, Frank!" Travis cried.

"Let it go!" Kinnard answered. "Follow it, that's the best we can do!"

The wind was behind the fires. Flames were shooting up from the tall, dry grass head high and advancing faster than a man could walk.

"This didn't start by accident, Kinnard!" Jesse shouted. "This fire was set!"

"You can be damn sure of that, Jesse! You give me a hand with hitching the team. We'll get the wagon across the river while there's time. Jamie, you and Rusty drive the cavvy across. You can make it if you hurry. The rest of us will try to stay with the herd."

Hitching the team did not take long. Kinnard handed the reins to Honey. "Get going!" he ordered. "There ain't enough water in the Tongue to bother you. When you get across, keep on going till you're beyond the fire. You'll be all right; it's moving this way; it ain't burning back."

Honey lashed the four-horse team and they crashed through the brush that choked the river bottom. Kinnard heard them strike the water and knew the wagon was safe. Jamie and Rusty ran the snorting remuda through the scrub in the wake of the wagon.

When Kinnard swung into the saddle, he found himself alone. The stampeding herd was a moving blur to the south with Buckmaster and the crew in hot pursuit. He took out after them at a driving gallop. To the east where the fire had the full force of the wind behind it, it was burning so fiercely that it was turning night into day. It was still a third of a mile away.

"It's running fast enough to close the gap in another ten to twelve minutes," he told himself. He knew this was Arnett's work. There was no other explanation. It was confirmed beyond doubt when he saw riders silhouetted in between the cattle and fire to the east. They were popping blankets as they raced alongside the panic-stricken herd, whipping it to even greater frenzy.

It was an old trick, but Kinnard did not immediately understand Arnett's purpose in employing it now. Its only effect could be to increase the speed at which the stampeding cattle were running and help to get them through the opening before the converging fires met and trapped them. It didn't make sense.

"My God!" Kinnard groaned as he recalled the country through which he had led the way that afternoon, sheer cliffs and steep bluffs. Arnett's intention was plain enough now. Setting the grass afire was only his way of stampeding the cows; fire might kill some of them, but the whole herd would be destroyed if it could be driven over the cliffs.

He shouted a warning to the crew. He couldn't be sure they heard. When he began firing at the silhouetted riders on the far side of the herd, Jesse and the others saw what he saw and set their guns to bucking. Kinnard couldn't tell what effect the shooting was having; the flames were nearer and the air was thick with smoke. When they got beyond the burning grass and the air cleared somewhat, he could see nothing of Arnett's riders. He caught up with Travis and Ike. The three of them tried desperately to get ahead of the herd and turn it. They found it impossible.

Travis was a bit off to the right. He was the first to see the leaders suddenly drop out of sight. His cry turned Kinnard and Buckmaster his way. They saw the second line go over. The cows weren't plunging blindly to their death as sheep will do; only the leaders had gone over that way; those that followed saw their danger and hesitated, but the weight of numbers behind them carried several hundred over.

The fire was far away now and would burn itself out in some lonely canyon. The first thing to do was to quiet what was left of the herd.

"You and the boys take care of that, Jesse," said

Kinnard. "I'll go back and see how Jamie and the others made out."

"This is awful!" Buckmaster groaned. "I can hear the stuff dyin' down there. It'll be mornin' before we know what the score is." He shook his head despondently. "We underestimated Arnett, Kinnard! There's nothin' that son of a bitch won't do!"

Kinnard could only nod in agreement. "He hurt us bad this time, Jesse. All we can do is make the best of it and limp along the rest of the way. I'll be back as soon as I can."

He found Jamie and the others none the worse for their experience. The horses were safe. The wagon had not fared as well. In the darkness, a wheel had struck a stump and cracked an axle. Honey didn't see how it could go on.

"We'll patch it up good enough to get us to Miles City," Kinnard told him. His account of what had happened stunned Jamie.

"Frank, it was Worth, wasn't it?"

"Who else would be interested in wiping us out. Certainly it was Arnett."

She wanted to return with him but he wouldn't have it.

When he returned to the herd, he found that it had been moved back from the cliff and was quieting down. Dawn was already in the air. With the coming of daylight, they found a trail off to the east that enabled them to reach the base of the cliff. Their loss was greater than they had estimated.

"We can put it at three hundred head and not be far wrong," Travis declared. "Everything that went over is either dead or will have to be destroyed."

It took them some time to finish the grisly task. Under a pile of cows, they found a horse, and a few feet away the crushed body of a man. He was beyond being recognized, but the brand, A in a box, on his horse was unmistakable evidence that they could charge up what had happened to Arnett.

They got the man out and covered the body with stones. They had no shovel; it was the best they could do.

"That bastard Arnett knows we're wise to him now," Ike Jarvis grunted savagely. "Montana ain't goin' to be big enough for him and us. You goin' after him, Frank?"

"No, I'll let him come to me. He'll keep out of the way for a time, but I'll locate him. I'll kill him or he'll kill me."

14

The best explanation given inquiring strangers who wondered why Miles City had been located so disadvantageously on the low east bank of the Tongue, where it was exposed to the ravages of that unpredictable river, was that the founders had wanted it there. Though it was getting old, old as age was reckoned in Montana Territory, there were still those who prophesied that it would be destroyed one day by high water and the ice gorges that formed in the Tongue. It had had several near-misses. But that had not kept it from prospering. The original site had been hacked out of a grove of big cottonwoods. Most of the old trees were gone. Of those that remained many were scarred and ragged, their bark ripped off by masses of crashing ice.

The bed-ground outside of town had been used so extensively in the past several weeks that when Kinnard saw it he realized that not even a goat could find a living there. It had sent him back to the outfit at once to order it held several miles up the Tongue.

"At least there's some grass here," he told Buckmaster. "We can keep the stuff on it until we're ready to cross the Tongue and the Yellowstone. If you buy what we need from Vic Stowell, he'll deliver out to the bed-ground and we can pick it up as we're passing. That'll save sending the wagon into town."

It made sense to Jesse. He asked about Arnett.

"He's evidently got his stuff across already, no sign of him."

The two of them rode into town a few minutes after nine the next morning. For Kinnard it was like coming home, in a way. He was as well-known in Miles City as Deadwood. The place had not changed in his absence. Hotel accommodations were still almost non-existent. Miles City laughed about it, claiming that its visitors did not come to eat and sleep. But a man with a thirst could find no fault with what it had to offer.

"We'll walk back to the bank and have a talk with Charlie Roberts," Kinnard said, as they put their horses up to the rack in front of Stowell's store. "We'll get some information from him."

What Roberts had to say was not encouraging.

"There's no point in making things better than they are," he said. "You want the truth, Frank."

"Naturally—"

"Then I got to tell you the situation looks bad. Beef prices are way down, but cattle are being shipped every day. As Milo Evans told me yesterday, he'd rather take what he can get now than wait till after roundup-time and have nothing but skin and bones to sell. Things are so bad up around Rocky Point that some of the owners are trying to get permission to send their stuff across the Missouri into the Fort Belknap Reservation. There was some rain in the Judith Basin a couple weeks ago. I understand it saved the grass. But it would be foolish to try to crowd in there; all that range is being used. The thousands of cattle that are coming up the trail ain't helping things a bit. You can't blame Montana stockmen if they feel that you fellows are taking the bread out of their mouths. It'll be a miracle if trouble doesn't develop somewhere."

"I don't know why it should," Jesse demurred. "This is a free-range country."

"It's free if you see it first and are strong enough to hold on to it," retorted Roberts. "I haven't seen your friend Con Gerstenberg in months, Frank. I guess he can buy whatever he needs in Lewistown. That town is growing fast and getting tough."

"That was bound to happen," Kinnard said with little interest. "By the way, Charlie, have you had business with any of the trail outfits that have been showing up?"

"With two or three—cashing checks and bank drafts. A man named Arnett was in day before yesterday. Had to have a check cashed. You acquainted with him?"

"Yeh. Did he give you an idea of what he had in mind?"

"No. I wouldn't ask him any sooner than I'd ask you. If you have a trick up your sleeve, Frank, that's the place to keep it."

They didn't linger long. When they were back on the street, Jesse said:

"That settles it. It's Flat Willow or bust for us."

"No question about it," Kinnard agreed.

He was stopped three or four times on the short walk back to Stowell's by old acquaintances. In the store, he introduced Buckmaster to the proprietor.

"While you're busy here, I'll step into that barbershop next to the bank, Jesse. If you get through before I do, look for me there."

Countless times he had sat in the chair in Casey Dunnigan's barbershop and amused himself by watching the passersby in the big mirror that covered most of the rear wall. Except when Casey got in the way, it was a grandstand seat from which the life of Miles City could be observed almost as well as on the street itself. Between watching the passing show and listening to Casey's endless chatter (he always had the news and scandal of the town at his tongue's end) it was an altogether pleasant experience to sit there and have your hair cut.

Kinnard recognized a score of familiar faces in the throng that passed. Casey had finished with the shears and was reaching for comb and brush, when Kinnard was electrified at sight of

Portugay moving up the sidewalk. Little Steve wasn't strolling; his face was twisted into a hard, set look, and his step was as deliberate and stiff-legged as though he were stalking someone.

It cried a warning to Kinnard. Tearing off the towel and sheet that Casey had spread over him, he leaped out of the chair.

"I'll be back," he told the startled Casey.

Clamping on his hat, he rushed to the door. Before he reached it two shots rang out down the street, followed by the rapidly receding clatter of a hard-running horse pounding out of town. There was nothing unusual about the firing of a gun on Miles City's main street. It happened right along. But this was different. Some sixth sense told him what had happened. When he busted through the door and glanced up the street, he saw a man stretched out on the sidewalk in front of Stowell's. Men were running up from three or four directions. Kinnard ran, too, though it wasn't necessary; he knew who it was on the sidewalk. When he pushed through the gathering group, his fears were confirmed; the man was dead, and it was Jesse Buckmaster.

A pink-cheeked man with an iron gray mustache knelt down beside him a few moments later and was surprised to see him. He was Tom Buckingham, the marshal of Miles City.

"Frank, I didn't know you were in town. You acquainted with this man?"

"My pardner, Tom. We came up from Oklahoma together."

"You got any idea who killed him?"

"A vicious little rat by the name of Steve Portugay."

He explained how he had seen little Steve pass the barbershop.

"He came within an inch of rubbing me out, back in Kansas. We had trouble with him all the way up."

Half a dozen men had witnessed the killing. They told the same story.

"Didn't they have any words at all?" the marshal asked.

"No, Tom, not a word," a bystander said. "The old man came out of the store and was so surprised at seein' the fella that he just stood there. The little runt whipped up his gun and let him have it—two quick shots."

"There was a lot of horses at the rail," another added. "He grabbed the nearest one—that buckskin of Mart Banion's—and raced up the street lickety hell."

"Too damn bad one of you didn't put a slug into him," Buckingham grunted. "You can give me his description later, Frank," he added as he straightened up. He picked out a man in the crowd. "Joe, run down to Hofaker's and tell him to get up here with his wagon right away."

Vic Stowell had hurried back into his store. He

came out with a piece of canvas and they covered the body.

"I'd just finished waiting on him, Frank," said Stowell. "What do you want me to do with the stuff he bought?"

"Hold it, Vic. We'll need it. I'll arrange with you about it later in the day."

Buckingham walked aside with Kinnard as they waited for the undertaker to arrive.

"No need to tell you, Frank. I'm sorry this happened. I know it's a blow to you."

"Nothing compared to what it'll be to his daughter. She's with us, Tom. I—I just don't know how to tell her. We'll have to go on. That'll make it even harder on her."

"Well, you can give him a decent burial. That's something. Hofaker can have the grave dug and take care of everything. I hope you got some idea where you're going to light with your stock."

"I have, Tom. It'll be spring, of course, before any money will be coming in. I may have to find a job."

"Would you be interested in policing a town like Lewistown?"

"Why, I don't know. Why do you ask?"

"Shad Bowles wants to turn in his badge. His health is so poor he can't go on much longer. They've asked me to recommend someone. You'd be a good man, Frank. You could ramrod that town. Suppose I give you a letter before you leave. Later on, if you're interested, you can go to Lewistown and talk to the Town Board."

"You can do that if you want," Kinnard told him. "Right now I'm going to have all I can do getting through today and tomorrow."

The undertaker took the body. They followed him to his establishment. Kinnard made a little bundle of Jesse's wallet, money-belt and gun. He remembered that he had not paid the barber. He gave Buckingham a dollar and asked him to take care of it.

"I'll be in this afternoon with his daughter and some of his old crew. I'll see you then, Tom."

The three miles back to the wagon was the longest ride Kinnard had ever made. Travis, old Ike and Rusty were out with the herd. He turned to them before going in and told them what had happened. Their first concern was for Jamie. If they had few words at their command with which to express their sympathy, no such handicap held them back when it came to voicing their wrath against Steve Portugay.

"We shoulda hung that little skunk as we planned!" Ike Jarvis growled. "She never shoulda let him git away!"

"Ike, I don't want you or anyone else to remind her of that." Kinnard's mouth had a stern, hard set. "She'll have enough to bear up under without anything of that sort. You've been with the

Buckmasters longer than any of us. You come in with me. Between us, maybe we can soften the blow a bit."

They tried valiantly but as always happens on such occasions, the ugly truth had to be told. Johnny Gaines and the others stood around, shifting feet, a stricken look on their homely faces. They wanted to help her, and it was more than just the usual cowboy loyalty to his outfit, but they were powerless.

"What am I going to do?" she sobbed. "What's to become of me?"

"We're going to stick together, Jamie, and go on," said Kinnard. "That's what your father would want. He wasn't the one they wanted to get; they missed me, so they got him."

Ike saw that she didn't understand. He tried to explain.

"Arnett pulled out in a hurry, knowin' we was only a day or so behind him, to throw us off guard. When he left that little rat behind in Miles City it was for jest one purpose—to gun Frank and your pa. We'll catch up with that pair someday."

"No matter how long it takes," Lin vowed.

"One of us will, even if I have to do it myself, missy," black Honey blubbered.

"That'll be my job," said Kinnard. "You do the cooking."

It was not until he saw that she had a grip on

herself that he gave her the little bundle he had brought out from the undertaker's. It broke her up again.

"I guess she'd like to be alone for a bit," said Kinnard. The others left and with his arm around her he led her under the trees and made her sit down.

"You're being awfully kind, Frank. This all seems like some terrible nightmare. But I know it isn't." A sob racked her and she couldn't go on.

"I thought we might go into town for an hour or two this afternoon," he suggested. "There's some details we'll have to settle. If we have the services in the morning, we can have Stowell's wagon meet us on the bed-ground in the afternoon with the supplies your father bought. We could be across the Yellowstone before evening."

She nodded woodenly. "Whatever you say, Frank." She looked up at him through her tears. "You and the boys are not saying anything but I know what you're thinking. If I hadn't interfered that night this would never have happened. How can I ever forgive myself?"

"You did what you thought was right—what you felt you had to do." His tone was as patient as it was grim. "I have to take some of the blame. I should never have let things go as far as I did. When the evidence against Portugay piled up, I shouldn't have waited; I should have gunned him at once and let it go at that. I blame myself for not sticking close to your father this morning—"

"You didn't know, Frank—"

"Neither did you. You get yourself straightened out now. We'll go in this afternoon."

The hours that followed were trying ones for Frank Kinnard, and not only on Jamie's account. She bore up better than he expected. What weighed heaviest was the new sense of responsibility that had devolved on him with the death of Jesse Buckmaster. He had been making the decisions for a long time, but there had always been some room to allow for mistakes. There was none now; he had to get her settled and see that she had at least a fair chance of making a living. In so dedicating himself to her welfare, he didn't have to search for a reason. He felt he owed her no less. If there were other reasons, more pertinent and more personal, he didn't explore them.

When the simple services were over and Jesse had been laid to rest in Miles City's fenced-in "burying-ground," he sent Jamie and Honey, and those members of the crew that could be spared to attend the funeral, back to the wagon with instructions to meet him on the bed-ground by noon at the latest. Tom Buckingham had come to the cemetery. The two of them rode back to town together.

"I was talking to a couple soldiers from the

fort this morning," said Buckingham. "They saw a rider crossing the river just before noon yesterday. From the description I got, it must have been this fella Portugay. They didn't pay much attention to him after he got across. They thought he was heading north."

"No doubt."

"You know there's nothing much I can do about snagging him, Frank. I'll keep my ears open. If he shows up in town, I'll take him into custody and charge him with murder. You keep in touch with me."

Before they parted, Buckingham gave him the letter he had promised.

"You may or may not care to use it."

The hot ruinous summer was gone. You could feel it in the air. In the early morning a blue haze hung in the sky. Larks and flickers were on the wing from dawn to sunset. They showed no inclination to flock up. Blackbirds were gathering already, not in the immense flocks in which they congregated for a week or two before migrating, but they were patently aware of the changing season. On the hillsides the clumps of aspen were still green, as were the thickets of wild plum and alders along the ravines. Kinnard knew it wouldn't be long now before they were turning to gold.

The Yellowstone was now seven days behind

them. They had seen no change in the country, high, rolling prairie, dotted with sage and greasewood and thinly carpeted with parched buffalo grass.

"It's beginning to look pretty discouraging," Jamie remarked that evening. It was the first complaint she had voiced. The death of her father had changed her in some intangible way; she was more mature, more womanly. She had done her work well and asked no favors.

They were camped a few miles east of the divide between the Yellowstone and the Musselshell.

"You'll see some changes tomorrow, as soon as we get over the divide," Kinnard told her. "Bluffs and broken country all the way to the river. We'll cross the Musselshell in the afternoon. We ought to see better grass soon after that."

From the crest of the divide they had an excellent view of the Little Snowies, off to the west. Sixty miles away, Kinnard said. They didn't seem half that far to Jamie. There were patches of snow on the peaks already; the lower slopes were black with pine and cedar.

"Flat Willow heads in those mountains," he explained. "We'll have to go around the long way to get there."

Kinnard had calculated that it would take them ten days to reach Flat Willow. That was hitting the nail on the head, for on the morning of the tenth day they were moving up the valley, three to four miles across. It was beautiful country, the creek thirty-five to forty feet wide, flowing over a gravelly bottom, the water cold and clear. On the slopes dense stands of yellow pine rose in serrated ranks. The grass began to get better. There was bluestem and Mexican bayonet on the benches. It lifted the spirits of all. Bunches of cattle were everywhere.

"It's almost too good to be true," thought Jamie. It was no less than what the others were thinking.

Honey was far ahead with the wagon. Rounding a bend, in the course of another mile, their rejoicing was turned to dismay. The wagon had been stopped. A line of riders, no less than fifteen, blocked the way.

Kinnard flung up a hand, halting the drive. Two riders moved forward and catching Honey's team, turned it around and sent the wagon rolling back down the valley. Jamie spurred up to Kinnard.

"Frank, you know what this means!" she cried in pathetic agitation.

"I'm afraid I do. But I don't intend to be ordered off without putting up an argument."

A horseman loped toward them and pulled up when he was in speaking distance. He was a man of undistinguished appearance, of medium size, with a dusty look and a round German face. Kinnard was unacquainted with him, but he had seen him on several occasions in Miles City, in the old days. He knew this was Gus Kohrs, the ex-butcher-boy who had made himself one of the Territory's leading stockmen.

"You folks will have to turn around," Kohrs announced. "We ain't lettin' nobody crowd into Flat Willow. We've turned back two or three outfits, the last one day before yesterday."

"That's being pretty high-handed, ain't it?" Kinnard inquired. "You don't own this range."

"No, by damn, we don't. But it's ours under the Customary Range Act, and that's good Territorial law. We want to be peaceable about this, mister, but if you want trouble you can have it."

And now a second horseman came hurrying toward them—a big man, with a frosty mustache and a booming voice.

"What's the matter, Gus?" he demanded. "They givin' you an argument?"

"I dunno yet—"

The newcomer swung his horse around and faced Kinnard. His mouth fell open with surprise.

"What the hell's the meanin' of this?" he cried. "What are you doing, Frank, tryin' to crowd in here with a bunch of cows?"

"Some of them belong to me, Con. The grass is all dead, east of the Musselshell. We got to dig in somewhere."

Gerstenberg couldn't get over it.

"This is a helluva note, Frank. I wish you'd

tried somewhere else. You musta known we was in here."

Kinnard nodded. "Old Stony Thompson told me. I didn't expect to get the cream of the crop, Con. I figured maybe we could latch on to what you and Kohrs didn't need. The leavings would satisfy us."

"No!" Kohrs said adamantly. "We ain't listenin' to anythin' like that."

Gerstenberg got his attention and they dropped back a few yards and indulged in an argument that lasted three or four minutes. When they returned, Con said:

"Is there grass enough between this flat and the mouth of the crick to satisfy you?"

"I think so—"

"Wal, we're going to let you have it. But the upper end of this flat is the deadline, Frank. Is that understood?"

"Yeh—"

"And we expect you to bar the door to any outfits that shows up from now on," Kohrs told him. "That's the only reason I'm agreein' to the deal. We'll back you up. If you can't handle it yourself, you git word to us in a hurry."

"That'll be fine," Kinnard told them. "And we're obliged to both of you."

15

With genuine satisfaction Kinnard could review what they had accomplished in their first month on Flat Willow; cabins and corrals had been built; they had made some crude furniture. What they couldn't make had been freighted down from Lewistown. The fall rains had helped the grass; the cattle were picking up.

Jamie shared his enthusiasm. They didn't own a square foot of land, but they were a going concern and getting their roots in the ground. Both realized how much they owed the crew. The effort the men had put forth was not conditioned by the wages they were making. It went far beyond that. But money was going out and nothing coming in. Though neither mentioned it it was a continuing shadow that was seldom out of their minds.

Only one Oklahoma outfit had tried to move in on them. It had been turned back with no more than a heated argument. Elk and white-tailed deer were plentiful. Smaller game abounded. All could say they were living high.

Kinnard had inquired in Lewistown about Arnett. No one could tell him anything. He was sure that wherever the Texan was he had Portugay with him.

After supper Kinnard usually sat down with Jamie on the pile of logs that were being split for winter firewood. There was more snow up on the peaks, but down in the valley the weather was still mild and pleasant, even in the evening. Fall had definitely come to Flat Willow. The aspens were fountains of gold amid the dark green of the pines. Long after the sun had left the valley it caught the tops of the Little Snowies, splashing them with vermilion. It was a spectacle that fascinated Jamie.

"It's beautiful, Frank," she murmured as they sat on the logs this evening. "How I wish Dad were here to enjoy it. You might not have thought so, but he had an eye for such things."

She often spoke of her father. He never tried to stop her, knowing that it eased the ache in her heart. The fortitude she had shown was a source of wonder to him.

As they sat there talking, they saw a rider coming down the valley. His size alone identified him.

"It's Mr. Gerstenberg, Frank."

"It's Con, sure enough," he agreed.

The big man had visited them several times, once with his wife. It was reassuring to know that they had such backing as their friendly interest guaranteed.

"Don't git up," Con boomed as he got out of the saddle. "I'll sit down and gass with you a bit.

I saw some of your stuff on the way down. It's beginnin' to look better."

"It does," Kinnard agreed. "We'll be all right if a lot of it don't get winter-killed."

"I wouldn't worry too much about that, Frank. At no time last year did we have more than six inches of snow on the ground. And it didn't last long. I'm goin' up to Lewistown tomorrow and on to Fort Maginnis and the telegraph. I want to find out how the market is. If beef is still down, Gus and I ain't goin' to ship this fall. We'll carry everythin' over till spring and take our chances."

He had more to say about winter conditions.

"Northern bred stock will paw down through a foot of snow to git at the grass. I don't know whether these critters of yours will have sense enough to do it; I don't suppose they ever saw any snow."

"Very little," Jamie was compelled to admit. "Frank thinks we ought to save the grass on those benches across the creek for winter feeding."

"By all means, mam. Put your hosses up there with 'em. If the snows set up in a crust, the hosses will break it up. I came to ask if there's anythin' you want from town. I'll be glad to fetch it. I'm goin' over the hills to McDonald Crick and cut off about ten miles, so I won't be passin' this way in the mornin'."

"There are one or two things," said Jamie, "I'll run inside and make a little list for you. And thank you so much for bothering, Mr. Gerstenberg."

"No bother, mam. Just bein' neighborly."

How nice it was, she thought, to have someone looking out for you. She knew she owed it all to Kinnard.

She left them. Con started to fill his pipe and stopped.

"She's an exceptional young woman, Frank."

"She is," the latter agreed.

He was not prepared for what followed, for with a directness that was characteristic with him, the big man said:

"Why don't the two of you git married?"

"Con, you're jumping the gun," Kinnard answered, doing his best to dissemble his embarrassment. "You know I'm a lone wolf."

"You mean you don't know if she'd have you—is that it?"

"Well," Kinnard laughed, "I imagine she'd have something to say about it." His manner changed suddenly and, dead sober, he added: "There's nothing like that between us, Con. I respect and admire her, but that's as far as it goes."

He was glad to have Jamie rejoin them and rescue him from Gerstenberg's impertinent chatter.

Con left as night fell.

"I like that man, Frank," said Jamie, when the two of them were alone. "He's so kind and so wise."

"Yeh," was his irascible answer. "And he can be a bit of a damn fool, too."

He had no intention of explaining what prompted the observation.

He had reminded her several times of the arrangement he had made with her father to pay his share of the expenses they incurred on the way north. It was only at his insistence that she finally gave him an accounting. He paid her at once. It left him strapped, a fact that he did not divulge to her. But once the subject of money had been broached it brought them face to face with hard realities.

"Frank, do you realize it's going to be eight to nine months before we can hope to have any money coming in?"

"I do," he nodded. "I been carrying that problem around in my mind for weeks."

"What are we going to do? Two-thirds of the cows belong to me. The only fair thing is to share expenses on that basis. But for the life of me I don't see how I can hold up my end for that long—paying out wages every month to five men, six if you include Honey, and he's almost indispensable."

"Have you said anything to them?"

"No, how could I? They're so far away from home and everyone they know. It would break my heart to turn them off, even one."

"I'll talk to them, and the sooner the better." He got up and took a turn around the room. "I'd rather have my arm cut off than do it; I feel about them just as you do. But we got to have an understanding. I'll bring it up tonight when they're all in the bunkhouse."

"Just what are you going to say, Frank?" she asked, her eyes troubled and appealing.

"I don't know exactly. They can't catch on with some other outfit with things so bad all across eastern Montana. You saw a lot of cow-hands standing around in Lewistown. They wouldn't be spending their time in town if they had a job."

He stopped at the window, with his back to her, and communed with himself for a moment.

"We might as well put it on the line, Jamie—tell them their money will be ready on the first of the month but after that they'll have to wait for their wages till we get on our feet. If they want to stick with us on those terms they can be sure of bed and grub. I don't know what else I can say."

He bunked with the crew. He called them around him and explained the situation, telling them what they could look forward to if they wanted to stick it out.

It struck him almost at once that what he was saying came as no surprise.

"Have you boys been talking this over behind my back?" he demanded acrimoniously.

"We have, Frank," Ike Jarvis replied. "You needn't git sore about it. We figgered money must be gittin' scarce and it was up to us to take some of the load off you and Jamie. There ain't no reason why we need cash on the barrel-head over the winter. We'll wait. The way we feel about the two of you ain't got nothin' to do with wages. We figgered you knew that."

Kinnard was touched. His glance ran from one to another.

"I see that goes for all of you," he said with a deep humility. "I don't know how to thank you. I can only say that if this little spread grows and amounts to something, you boys will be well taken care of." He opened the door and looked across at Jamie's cabin. "She's still up. I'll walk over and tell her how you feel. She'll sleep better for knowing."

As the days passed, the conviction grew on Kinnard that he could be spared from the ranch till spring. He had done nothing about the letter Tom Buckingham had given him. He felt if the job were still open that he should take it; it would enable him to replenish his own purse and at the same time make sure that Jamie had money enough to keep the ranch going.

When he told her one evening that he was going up to Lewistown for a day or two, he said nothing about his plans, thinking to spare her any disappointment she might feel if they failed to materialize.

When he returned, she saw as soon as he walked into her cabin that he was in high spirits. She was sitting at the table that stood in the center of the room, busy with needle and thread, binding off a blanket.

"Frank, you've had good news!" she cried. "I can see it sticking out all over you. What is it?"

"I got a job, Jamie," he replied, sitting down across the table from her. "You remember the letter Tom Buckingham gave me?"

"Yes—"

"Well, I saw the Board and they've appointed me marshal of the town. I'm taking over the first of the week."

She dropped her work and stared at him aghast.

"Frank, why did you do it? That's a dangerous job—"

"That part of it doesn't amount to anything. We'll have money enough to keep on going. We can quit worrying."

"You mean you can. What about me? I don't care what you say, I know what that town will be like when winter closes down and it fills up with tough characters. You'll be new. Some fool who thinks he's got a fast gun will try to down you and make a reputation for himself."

"Please, Jamie, don't get yourself worked up over nothing," he pleaded. "Shad Bowles has worn the badge for years. He's getting on; he's sick; that's the only reason he's retiring. As for that fast gun business, it's mostly a lot of nonsense. Nine out of ten of these fast gunmen are just saloon punks. They're dangerous if you let them get close to you; at twenty feet, a man with a cool head and a steady hand will down them every time."

She listened patiently to all he had to say but it was without effect on her.

"I don't like it," she said very positively. "And I don't like the way you went about it—saying nothing until it was an accomplished fact. You could have spoken to me."

"I was afraid I might not get the job. I thought you'd be all for it if I did. It's going to mean something to us to have a few hundred dollars extra next spring. We can spread out. The grass will come good; we can put some stock along the river or even up McDonald Creek. We'll buy northern bred stock. Con will have a lot of stuff to sell. You do want to go on and build up the outfit, don't you?"

"You know I do. You don't have to ask." She was still provoked with him. "You'll be away all winter. You expect me to run the ranch by myself?"

"Don't put it that way," he said on a rising note of impatience. "You'll have the crew here to look out for you. If anything unexpected comes up, talk it over with Jim Travis. You can depend on Jim; he's got good judgment. If you have to get in touch with me, Lewistown ain't so far away. I figure I can get down once in a while. You can come up if you care to. If you do, I don't want you to set out alone, Jamie. I want you to remember that. You get Jim to go up with you."

"Why do you say that?" she asked, alarmed by his sudden gravity.

"Because I believe Arnett has holed in somewhere west of the Musselshell. Wherever he is, we can be pretty sure Portugay is with him. I don't know whether they'd harm you or not, but I don't want you to run into them."

It turned her thoughts in another direction. She did not immediately have anything to say, but when she spoke, her vexation was gone; if he could think of her danger, she could think of his.

"Wherever they are, Frank, they'll learn quickly enough that you're Lewistown's town marshal. It'll draw them to you just as surely as molasses draws flies."

"I hope so," was his flat answer.

"Was that in the back of your mind when you took the job?"

"I suppose it was. I swore I'd hunt them down. I haven't forgotten. When I think of your father lying dead there on the sidewalk in Miles City, and all the trouble they made us on the way north, and how close they came to putting me under, I know what I'll do when I meet up with them."

"But you'll be a peace officer. You can't kill them without a warning—"

"I'll give them the same warning they gave your father and me—and that was none at all."

Lewistown was only half the size of Miles City. But it was doing all right for a town that had yet to hear the mournful wail of a diamond stack steam locomotive or see a plume of smoke trailing across the sky from an east-bound stock train. That would come with time. Meanwhile money had been raised to build a telegraph line to connect with the military telegraph at Fort Maginnis. The consent of the War Department was necessary. The Honorable Martin Feeney, Montana's territorial delegate to the Congress, was pressing the matter, in far-away Washington.

Kinnard found it quite like other towns he had known. Business-wise, it was a one-street town, wide open and, as Tom Buckingham had said, getting tough. He knew before he had been on the job twenty-four hours that the town as a whole was reserving judgment on him, waiting for him to prove himself before they took him seriously; as always when it had a new man wearing the badge, the saloon element would find a way to test his mettle. He kept it in mind as he patrolled the street, knowing that when his hand was forced he would have to stand up to it or the town would get away from him and he'd be gun-bait for every gun-toter who rode in.

It came sooner than he expected. It was the middle of the afternoon when a man ran into his office to tell him a fight had broken out in the Buckhorn saloon and the place was being wrecked. The saloon was a hangout for cowboys and soldiers down from Maginnis for a bust.

When he walked in the Buckhorn was a shambles, tables and chairs overturned and the floor strewn with playing cards. A dozen men were lined up at the bar watching the fight. He paused as though watching it, too, but it was the men at the bar on whom his eyes were really fixed. When he saw that their attention was now directed at him and that they no longer had any interest in the grunting, heaving pair that were swinging ineffectually at one another and not doing any damage, the suspicion turned to certainty in his mind that this was a staged affair, put on for the purpose of seeing what he would do about it. It gave him his cue. He turned to the struggling pair.

"You gladiators better begin throwing some punches before you wear yourselves out," he advised with a derisive laugh. "If you're counting on me to stop this fake fight, you got another guess coming."

Someone at the bar laughed and the others took it up. The fighters stopped their nonsense.

"Come on have a drink, Marshal," one of them invited. "You're all right, Kinnard; we jest wanted to see how much savvy you had."

It was a good joke. The town laughed about it for a day. But the roughs of Lewistown weren't satisfied; they wanted further evidence that the new marshal had to be taken seriously. They got it on Saturday morning, always the busiest day of the week. Kinnard was in Powers' general store when the shooting began. He hurried to the door with Powers. Out in the middle of the street in front of Crowley's Hotel, a man, apparently well liquored, was amusing himself by shooting at the wooden birds that formed part of the ornate railing of the hotel's second story veranda.

"Who is he?" Kinnard asked.

"Coley Davis, a Judith River puncher. He's dangerous when he's drunk, Marshal. Watch yourself."

Kinnard knew his hand was being called. When he stepped out into the street, half a hundred men were watching to see what he would do. Coley saw him coming but let it make no difference to him. He reloaded his gun and went on with his target practice. He was either not as drunk as he seemed or an expert shot; every time he fired, he shattered one of Crowley's wooden birds.

Kinnard came down the middle of the street and stopped twenty feet away.

"Coley, I'm arresting you for disturbing the

peace," he called out. "Throw away your gun."

"Like hell!" he was told. "You want my gun, come and git it."

Knowing he had an audience, and being a showoff at heart, he took aim on another bird. With a quickness that startled the onlookers, and they were not inexperienced at such things, Kinnard drew and fired. Coley Davis's gun went flying out of his mangled hand.

Kinnard could have killed him, as those who watched expected him to do; he had the provocation and authority for it. That he chose another way impressed them far more than a killing.

He picked up the man's pistol and marched him off to a doctor before locking him up.

It ended speculation about Kinnard. Lewistown had seen and it was convinced. He began to feel at home. Primarily he was responsible only for the peace of the town and the safety of its citizens. He found the task not too difficult. He was soon on friendly terms with leading business men and its elected officials. He took a drink when he pleased, but he did not gamble; for the first time in his life money really meant something to him and it was not to be risked at cards. He promised himself that, barring some unforeseen set-back on Flat Willow, he would have not less than a thousand dollars in the bank by the time spring rolled around.

He expected that in a place the size of Lewistown he would find at least some acquaintances of other days in Deadwood and Miles City. He didn't have to look for them; they found him. If on moral grounds one of them had to be regarded as undesirable, he could not bring himself to turn his back on her, for she it was who had warned him that Sheriff Tim Grady and his gang were about to frame him for murder. But he was now in the public eye and what he did and with whom he associated did not go unnoticed, especially by the so-called "good women" of the town.

No less than seven prominent stockmen, Con Gerstenberg among them, had established permanent homes in Lewistown. Their wives formed the backbone of Lewistown "society." They read papers on art and literature at their weekly get-togethers and labored indefatigably in the twin causes of culture and decency.

No one worked harder at keeping a very wide gulf between women of good repute, such as herself (she was an immense woman, well over fifty and presumably safe from personal temptation) and the soiled doves who inhabited a certain section of town, than Frieda Gerstenberg. She felt it to be her duty to spend a week now and then on Flat Willow with Con.

Though she had met Jamie only once, she had been favorably impressed. She had not mentioned her to her friends but she did so this afternoon when they gathered over the coffee cups and a three-layer cake in her dining room and took aim on Kinnard. She painted a pathetic picture of Jamie, alone in the world, living in a one-room, dirt floor cabin and doing a man's work in keeping the outfit together.

"I don't know what she and this man Kinnard would have done if Con and Mr. K. hadn't allowed them to move into Flat Willow."

"That's the way Joe and I started, in a one-room cabin," little Mrs. Cora May Pulverson observed rather tartly. "Nothing so remarkable about that. Of course we was married. It's mighty peculiar the two of them just being partners."

"She's a lady, Cora," Mrs. Gerstenberg informed her, understanding the insinuation. "You always can tell. Con says there's nothing between them, just business. But I ain't foolish enough to believe that. I think the child is in love with Kinnard. That's what infuriates me when I see how he's carrying on with that Belle Hart woman."

Just to hear the name made them see red. Buxom Belle Hart was Lewistown's most prosperous "madam." It was their sworn resolve not to be content until she and her strumpets had been run out of town.

"It's common knowledge that he visits her place," the Reverend Mrs. Cutbill remarked.

"If that was all, Nettie!" Frieda Gerstenberg squared her generous shoulders militantly. "He's so brazen. You all know how she drives about downtown in the afternoon in that buggy with the yellow wheels. I actually saw her stopped in front of Powers' store yesterday and him out there in the middle of the street talking to her. I tell you, ladies, someone should speak to him."

"I did, Frieda," said Cora May. "He as good as told me to mind my own business. I think we should let Miss Buckmaster know how he's behaving."

There was a chorus of agreement.

"You're the one to tell her, Frieda," the Reverend Mrs. Cutbill declared. "You'll be going down to Flat Willow before the Fall Fair, won't you?"

"I wasn't going down, but I think I will." Frieda Gerstenberg assumed a martyr's pose. "I think it's my Christian duty to speak to that child."

16

Though this was only the fourth year of the annual Lewistown Fair (a parade and horse racing in the afternoon, fireworks at night) it had become something of an institution. It brought people in from a hundred miles around. It meant business for the merchants, saloonkeepers and other purveyors of entertainment, such as Belle Hart. Since they put up the money that made the affair possible, their wishes had to be considered, and they refused to be deterred by the feeling in some quarters that with all of eastern Montana feeling the pinch of the drought and many stockmen facing disaster, the Fair should not be held this year. That was a foolish argument, they contended; when conditions were bad, men needed a holiday and a little excitement more than ever that they might get their minds off their troubles.

The Town Board, which they controlled, went along with their plans to make the fair bigger and better than ever. That august body called Kinnard to a meeting and informed him that they were giving him a temporary deputy, a young man named Will Scott, who had served in that capacity before.

"Frank, you got things under control," Powers said as the two of them left the meeting together.

"If you want to ride down to Flat Willow for a day there's no reason why you can't do it. You needn't worry about Scott; he's capable."

Kinnard was happy to take advantage of the opportunity. He had news for Jamie, but that hardly explained his eagerness to see her. Unaware of Frieda Gerstenberg's meddling and what awaited him, he took the shortcut across the hills from McDonald's Creek to Flat Willow.

When the elephantine Mrs. Gerstenberg had brought her scandalous tale to Jamie, the latter had insisted vehemently that Kinnard's morals and personal life were no concern of hers. It was a rather convincing performance, and when big Frieda returned up the valley to the Gerstenberg ranch she was of half a mind to accept it as the truth. In any event, she could console herself with the thought that she had done her duty. As for Jamie, she no sooner found herself alone than she flung herself on the bed and gave way to jealous rage. She told herself that she could never forgive Kinnard for shaming her in such fashion.

Racked with misery, she sobbed her eyes out. Something akin to terror gripped her when she realized she had spoken the truth when she said she had no claim on him. It seemed incredible. She knew now what she had known for weeks; she could deny it no longer; she loved him. Whether she meant anything to him or not, she loved him.

"He can't care for me—not that way," she sobbed. "He can't even have any respect for me—to take up with a person like that, the most notorious woman in Lewistown! At least he could have spared me that!"

Honey brought over her supper. She told him to put it on the table. He saw that she had been crying.

"Sunthin' wrong, missy?" he asked, always unfailingly solicitous.

"No, just having a good cry," she told him. "I'll be all right."

She did not attempt to eat anything. She put out the light and went to bed, her head splitting. In spite of the turmoil that raged in her mind, she saw with terrifying clarity that they could not go on together. He had made her position impossible; if the bank in Lewistown would loan her money on her cattle, she would buy him out. Or he would have to buy her out. If the latter was the case, she would go back to Texas, where she was known, and get a job.

"I couldn't stay here," she moaned. "It would kill me!"

Kinnard was there the next day but one. He arrived shortly after noon. She had herself in hand, but the strain she had been under for the past two days had left its mark on her. He noticed how pale her face was.

"You've been working too hard, Jamie," said

he, frankly concerned. "You don't look good. You're thin. You sure you're not sick?"

"No, I'm not sick," she replied, cool and distant. "Everything is fine here."

"I'm glad to hear that," he said, sensing from her tone that something was wrong. "I have some news for you."

"I have some for you, too, Frank," she informed him, drawing herself up proudly. "Perhaps I should give you mine first. I've had time enough to think it over and be sure what I want to say. It's simply this, Frank: we've come to the parting of the ways. Some arrangement will have to be made so that I can buy you out or you can buy me out."

"You can't mean that, Jamie." He couldn't believe his ears.

"But I do," she insisted. "It never occurred to me until the other day that our relationship had become the subject of range gossip. I blame myself for not realizing long ago that some ugly interpretations would be put on it."

"My God," he groaned, sinking into a chair, "this knocks the wind out of me; I don't know what to say. I know it's nonsense. I'll grant you it ain't the usual thing for a man and a woman to be pardners in a spread. But there ain't nothing wrong about it. Anyone who knows the circumstances that threw us together would understand."

Amazement had passed and angry indignation

whipped through him. It pulled him to his feet.

"Who's been running to you with that lying tale?"

"You're in Lewistown; you should know what the talk is—pitying me for being discarded in favor of such a person as this Belle Hart. I understand she isn't even young."

"Good God, so that's it!" he groaned. "Listen here, Jamie: no man would stoop to filling you full of that sort of talk; this is a woman's work. Frieda Gerstenberg has been down here. It was she, wasn't it?"

"Don't misunderstand me, Frank," she said icily. "I have no claim on you; you're free to do as you please. I just want my name kept out of your affairs. Can you borrow the money to buy me out?"

"I don't know," he answered, his face white with fury. "If that's what you want, I'll try."

"Perhaps your friend Miss Hart would accommodate you," she suggested with devastating effect.

"Shut up, you little fool!" he raged. "There's some things you'd better understand. I'm not having any affair with Belle Hart. I've known her for years; she's been a good friend to me. I can thank her that I'm alive. I told you how Grady tried to frame me in Deadwood. It was Belle who got the warning to me, or I never would have got away."

"I'm not asking for an explanation," Jamie said with haughty indifference.

"Well, by God, you're going to get one and listen to it. Belle's what she is and she don't pretend to be anything else. I can't turn my back on her for you or anyone. She can help me. She's done it already; she can get information that I could never get. It might interest you to know she's located your old friend Arnett and Steve Portugay for me. They're holed in down the Musselshell at the mouth of Bottle Creek—no grass—half his herd dead already. He blames his misfortunes on me."

The whereabouts of Arnett and Portugay should have been important to her, but she was so consumed with unreasoning rage and jealousy that she refused to show more than a superficial interest. Wanting to hurt him, she said with cutting sarcasm:

"I presume you'll do something about it—if you can tear yourself away from Miss Hart long enough."

Kinnard's self-control, already strained to the breaking point, snapped completely.

"To hell with you!" he cried. "I've had enough! I used to think you had some brains—that you were different. I was even idiot enough to think I was in love with you. I was going to ask you to be my wife."

She shuddered at his scornful laugh.

"Thank God, I got my eyes open in time!" he went on. "I'll buy you out. I'll find the money somewhere."

"Frank—!" she cried as he slammed out of the cabin.

She got the door open and ran out after him.

"Frank, come back!" she cried.

He was in the saddle and pounding away. Through her tears she saw him pull up a quarter of a mile away and speak briefly with Jim Travis. He was gone then. Crushed, utterly miserable, she turned back into the cabin . . . He loved her. And it had come to this! He wanted to marry her!

She was seized with a wild impulse to have a horse saddled and follow him back to Lewistown. A flash of sense stopped her; she didn't know the way, and he had warned never to make the trip alone.

She got through the long afternoon somehow. After supper she called Travis to the house and asked him what Kinnard had said.

"He told me Arnett and Portugay were down the river at Bottle Creek. He's afraid if we all go in to the fair next week they may run off most of our stock while we're gone. He made me promise that nobody goes to town."

He could see how depressed she was. Coupled with the brevity of Kinnard's visit, he was in no doubt that they had quarreled.

"I spoke to the boys a few minutes ago," he

continued. "They took it pretty hard; they had been counting on getting in to the races."

She was silent for a moment or two, feeling the stab of a new thrust of jealousy. "I wonder what his real reason is for not wanting us in Lewistown."

Travis' brows knitted in a quick frown. "What do you mean?"

"Nothing—nothing," she snapped. "I was just thinking out loud. When the time comes, I'll decide whether or not we go in to the fair."

The week passed without any word from Kinnard. It was Sunday again. In the bunkhouse the Lewistown Fair was the sole topic of conversation that evening. The nights were becoming cool enough to make a fire feel good. The men were gathered around the stove.

"Time's gittin' short," Ike Jarvis remarked. "The races is day after tomorrow. How do our chances of makin' it look to you, Jim?" he asked, addressing himself to Travis.

"I don't know. She's said nothing further to me. When I was over this afternoon, she had a dress laid out and was doing some sewing on it. I got the idea that she was figuring on wearing it to town. I didn't ask. She's still got her nose up in the air."

"The fight her and Frank had musta been a stem-winder," said Johnny. "I never knew her to hold a grudge for three or four days. It kinda puts us in a spot."

"It does," Travis agreed. "Frank laid down the law to me. I wouldn't like to cross him. He said to stay with the stuff. I figure that's what we ought to do. If she means to show him that he ain't bossing her, that's her business. Speaking for myself, I won't go to town unless she orders me to."

On Monday evening Jamie made known her decision to Travis.

"There's no reason why some of you shouldn't go in, Jim. I mean to go. You have the men draw straws to see which two stay here."

"If it's just the same to you, I'll be one of the two to stay," he told her. "I've always taken Frank's orders. I don't want to cross him."

"Well," she exclaimed with a little toss of her head, "I'm sorry I can't oblige you. You'll go with me."

"Is that an order, mam?" he asked after a moment's hesitation.

"It's an order."

She and the whole crew were at the corral in the morning, getting ready to leave—Johnny and Ike had lost out in the drawing—when they saw a rider coming up the creek. Even at a distance they could see that he was an emaciated old man who wore his hair long. Jamie's first thought was that it was Stony Thompson, the old-timer they had encountered on the Little Powder. It wasn't

Stony. Rusty Johnson was first to recognize him.

"It's Cim Smith," he told them. "He came up from the Canadian with Arnett."

"It is," Travis agreed. "He must have been in a fight; he's got a rag tied around his head."

"Why is he coming here?" Jamie asked. It was what the others were asking themselves.

"I can't imagine," was Jim's puzzled answer. "Suppose we wait for him to tell us."

The old Army scout rode up to them. Though the morning was cool, his horse was damp with sweat, indicating that he had come some distance and without losing any time.

"Howdy!" he greeted them, throwing up a hand. "Yuh know who I am?"

"We do," Travis acknowledged. There were blood stains on the rag tied around the visitor's head. "Looks like you'd had some trouble."

"Yeh. Arnett slapped me around some when I struck him for the money he's been holdin' back on me. I mean to be back in Texas before the snow comes." He looked them over with his faded eyes. "I knew I'd find yuh here. That's another thing Arnett holds agin yuh; we tried Flat Willow and got turned back."

Travis exchanged a glance with Jamie.

"You do the talking, Jim. Find out what he wants."

He didn't have to ask.

"I'll tell yuh why I'm here," Cim volunteered,

"and it won't take long. Arnett and that little snake who does his dirty work are on their way into Lewistown—and not to take in the fair. They're goin' to git Kinnard. They figger there'll be a lot of excitement and he'll have his hands full. Jest when he's arrestin' some drunk, they mean to let him have it. They got it all planned; if Portugay can't fetch him, Arnett will."

Fear clamped its icy fingers on Jamie. Anger and jealous exasperation were suddenly gone from her and she could think only of flying to Kinnard's side.

"What makes you so sure of what you say?" she demanded excitedly.

"I heard 'em talking, mam. Yuh can do what yuh please about it. I jest figgered yuh'd like to know."

The hawk-faced old man swung his horse and loped away. Jamie didn't waste a thought on him.

"We haven't a minute to lose," she cried. "Jim, can you find the short-cut Mr. Gerstenberg uses?"

"We can stop at the house and they'll tell us how to find it." Travis gave no indication that he was ready to rush off blindly. "It's a long ride; we couldn't be in town till early afternoon. We better give this some thought before we go busting off to Lewistown on Cim Smith's say-so."

"Good Lord, Jim, how can you say that?" Jamie burst out. "We've got to warn Frank. This isn't to be any gunfight; they intend to murder him!"

"That's right if we can take the old man's word for it. I don't know whether we should or not. Arnett could have sent him here with his story. That bloody rag he's got around his head could be a fake. The whole thing could be a shrewd trick to get us off the place. Frank was afraid Arnett might try something like that."

She didn't know what to say; Travis had suggested something that had not occurred to her. Though she was determined that nothing should stand in the way of her going to Lewistown, she could not brush aside his thought; its possibilities were too ominous for that.

"Oh, if I only knew the truth! What can we do, Jim?"

"Take Rusty with you," he advised. "The two of you go; the rest of us will stay here. You can find Frank and tell him why you're there. If Arnett shows up, we'll be ready for him."

That arrangement satisfied Jamie. Travis spoke to Rusty Johnson and the latter ran to the bunkhouse. He came back buckling on his gun-belt and carrying a rifle, which he slipped into his saddle boot. She eyed these preparations with some misgiving.

"Is that rifle necessary, Jim?"

"I don't believe it is but no harm can come from playing it safe. You stop at Gerstenberg's and they'll give you directions."

17

By the time the parade, led by young Bob Coles, the banker's son, costumed to represent Uncle Sam, replete with false hair and high hat, moved down the main street, the promoters of the fair could congratulate themselves on their judgment in holding it. No less than four hundred men and women were already in town, and more were still arriving, and that did not include the score of blanket Indians, down from the reservation, who sat immovable on the plank sidewalk.

The street presented a gala appearance; flags flying and the stores and saloons draped with bunting. Hawkers, who followed such affairs, were on hand, selling their wares. An itinerant photographer had set up his tent in the open space between the Buckhorn saloon and Sholz' bakery and was doing a rushing business. Ladies from the town's three rival churches who had taken advantage of the occasion to raise funds for their special needs, had established themselves on the several vacant lots in the block, where from long tables they were dispensing sandwiches and coffee.

It was a noisy, boisterous crowd, with a spattering of drunks even at that early hour but not yet threatening to get out of hand. After the parade, Kinnard walked back to his office and sat down with Will Scott, his deputy.

"Went off pretty good," said the latter. "No sign of trouble yet."

"It's early, Will. We're likely to have our hands full after the races." Kinnard took out his watch. "Maybe I better go to dinner; you can eat when I get back."

He had returned and was lounging in the doorway, keeping an eye on the street, when he was startled to see Jamie and Rusty flashing toward him on their lathered broncs. They had had no difficulty in cutting across to McDonald Creek from Flat Willow. After driving up its narrow valley for eighteen miles they had struck a well-defined road, used by Gerstenberg, Kohrs and other stockmen to the south, that led them to town. It was nearing two o'clock now. They had made the long ride in six and a half hours. The crowd was beginning to move out to the race track.

"What's the meaning of this?" Kinnard demanded, short and gruff. "I told Travis to be sure nobody left the ranch."

Jamie could see how angry he was at having his will crossed. It struck her as a shameful reward for her hours of anxiety.

"I'm here on your account," she said, resentment whipping through her. "You might have the courtesy to ask me to get down."

"I'm not asking you to sit there," he returned irascibly. "Get down and step inside."

Kinnard backed up against the desk but did not sit down. She didn't know how she had expected to be received. Certainly not with this churlish animosity.

"We had a visitor this morning—Cimmaron Smith, the old Scout who brought Worth Arnett up from Oklahoma," she began, her voice charged with suppressed anger. "They've had a fight. He told us Worth and Portugay left for Lewistown last evening—that they mean to kill you."

"Is that so?" he said skeptically. "You better tell me the whole story."

She gave it to him word for word. Even as she spoke, she could feel the impatience with which he waited for her to finish. The scornful set of his mouth left her in no doubt as to what he thought about it.

"Is that all?" he inquired with what she took for maddening indifference.

"Yes, that's all," she replied cuttingly, his assumption of superiority making her see red. "Obviously it doesn't mean anything to you."

"I wouldn't say that but I don't propose to get as worked up about it as you are. When Travis suggested that it was just a trick to get you all riding into town to save my skin, he had it sized up correctly. If you'd had your way about it, you wouldn't have found much left when you got back to Flat Willow. Thank God, he had the good sense to see through it. I don't think there's anything to worry about. When Arnett discovers that his game didn't work, he'll turn around with his bunch and go back down the river."

"And you don't think you're in any danger?" she demanded caustically.

"I don't know," he answered on a more sober note. "I'm prepared for trouble. If that pair are in town gunning for me, I'm not going to go in hiding. It wasn't necessary for you to put yourself out on my account. I can look out for myself."

Beside herself with fury, she leaped to her feet and started for the door.

"How despicable can you be?" she cried. "Gratitude from you I knew I wouldn't get. But I didn't expect to be slapped in the face for my trouble . . . Have you done anything about getting a loan?"

"Not yet—"

"Then I shall. I'll get a room at the hotel and stay in town overnight. I'll go to the bank in the morning."

"I won't stand in your way," he said woodenly. "Any arrangement you make will be satisfactory. I'm as anxious to be through with you as you are with me."

It was a monstrous lie. He realized it the moment she was gone. Say what he would, he knew she was the beginning and end of everything for him. He flung himself into his chair and scowled out his anger.

"The headstrong little brat, I'd like to spank her!" he thought.

If he had made light of the warning she had given him, it was largely on her account. He hadn't seen anything of Arnett and Portugay. But they well might be in town. If they were, he knew they were there for only one purpose.

The deputy marshal came back from dinner.

"You better ride out to the track and keep an eye on things there, Will," Kinnard told him. "I'll watch this end."

His face had a tightness that the other noticed. "Is there somethin' in the wind, Frank?" he asked, giving him a sharp glance.

"Nothing in particular."

After the other left, Kinnard tied down his holster, something he rarely did. He started down the street then. It looked the same as it had that morning, but he was keenly aware that the next few hours were pregnant with some ugly possibilities.

A loud knocking at the door aroused Jamie. Rusty had asked permission to take in the races. She had told him to go. She was so exhausted physically and mentally that she had soon cried herself to sleep. The afternoon had slipped away and the noise on the street below told her the crowd was streaming back from the track. When she opened the door, a big, buxom, tightly-corseted woman, violently blonde and smelling heavily of musk, stood there. Jamie's intuition told her immediately that the woman was Belle Hart.

"I've got to talk to you for a minute, Miss Buckmaster," said Belle. "May I come in?"

Jamie was too startled to do anything but nod her head in assent. Belle introduced herself. She sat down without waiting to be asked.

"I understand I'm responsible for the feuding going on between Frank and you. I'm here to set you straight."

"If I may ask," Jamie said as she recovered her wits, "how did you know I was in town and where to find me?"

"Nothing much happens in Lewistown, dearie, that doesn't get to me in a hurry," her visitor informed her with a self-satisfied smile. "Let me say that I've known Frank Kinnard for years. Since you're acquainted with the business I'm in, I ain't surprised that you can't believe the relations between Frank and me are what you might call decent. But that's what they are; there's never been anything sexy or romantic between us. I know a lot more about men than you do. Most of them are rotten; he's one of the few decent ones."

"He must be if he stoops to discussing me with another woman," Jamie returned with biting sarcasm.

"He's just a man, not an angel. He had to unburden himself to someone. You're young, Miss Buckmaster. That's no excuse for acting like a headstrong little fool. Frank's devoted to you. He had a right to expect you to have a little faith in him."

It was too much for Jamie. "I refuse to have you sit there and insult me, Miss Hart," she said with trembling voice. "I'll thank you to leave."

Belle was impervious to such tantrums. She settled back in her expensive finery and admired her imported Watteau stockings. She was now in her middle forties and though her face was raddled there was evidence left that she had once been a beautiful woman.

"I've seen too much of life to have any illusions left, dearie." Her tone was sober and profound. "You're young; you got yours left—or most of them. Hang on to them—hang on to them even if you have to lie to yourself. If they go, you'll never be happy. If Frank means anything to you—and I can see that he does—you patch up your quarrel with him before you leave town. You can't do it if you keep your nose up in the air and stand on your dignity. He'll meet you halfway if you give him a chance."

Jamie turned away to hide her agitation and

fight back her tears. She walked to the window. She could hear the street noises below but see nothing because of the intervening veranda that extended over the sidewalk. She wanted to tell Belle that she wasn't interested in her advice. If she didn't, it was because she realized how cheap and meaningless it would have been. As indignation ran out of her, embarrassment took its place. To her amazement, she said falteringly:

"I appreciate your coming to see me. I'm young, but I'm no child, Miss Hart. I came all the way from Flat Willow this morning to warn him that two men were in town to kill him. It meant nothing to him. He practically laughed in my face. He was furious because I was in town. About a week ago he told my foreman that nobody was to come in for the fair. I had disobeyed him. That was all that mattered to him."

"Perhaps it was his way of not letting you see how concerned he was."

"I can't believe it! According to him it was just a trick—they weren't in Lewistown—"

"They're here," said Belle. "He knows. I got word to him a few minutes ago."

Jamie was across the room in a flash. Her awe of Belle forgotten, she faced her with challenging eyes.

"If you know this town so well, where are those two men hiding?"

Belle shook her head. "I wish I knew. You get a

grip on yourself. Frank will make out. I'm betting on him. You stay here. This is a busy day for me. I'll be getting back to—"

That was as far as she got when a shot on the street stopped her. It was followed by spattering gunfire.

"My God, there it is!" she cried. "Come on, quick!"

She caught Jamie's hand and they ran out on the veranda.

Thirty minutes after the last race had been decided and bets paid, the crowd was back in town, largely congregated in one block. The sidewalks were jammed and the saloons bulging. In the popular Buckhorn, men stood three deep at the bar, the winners celebrating their good fortune and the losers doing their best to drown their bad luck.

It was almost as difficult to get out of the Buckhorn as it was to get in. Two of the fortunate ones, punchers in from the Judith River country, imbued with the laudable intention of spreading their winnings around a bit, managed to stagger through its bat-wing doors. They were usually harmless men, but it was their day to howl and they split the air with their shrill yipping, not minding the jostling of the crowd that forced them across the sidewalk into the street.

What followed began as nothing more serious

than drunken cowboy fun. Young Bob Coles, still wearing his Uncle Sam costume, was crossing the street, making for Powers' store, when he attracted their attention. It was the work of a second for one of them to whip up his gun and put a bullet through the boy's tall hat. As it went flying off his head, the other started his gun to bucking, the slugs kicking up little spurts of dust at Coles' feet. Panic stricken, the lad bolted for Powers' door, the sidewalk crowd parting to let him through. The jokesters howled with glee. But their amusement was cut short. Henry Coles, young Bob's elder brother, charged out of the store, a pistol in his hand. Before anyone could stop him, he downed one of the two men and wounded the other.

Jamie and Belle were in time to see it. The sidewalk was suddenly clear and the street empty. Jamie felt nausea overcoming her; never before had she seen a man killed and another wounded.

"The damn fools!" Belle groaned. "Crazy drunk!" She felt Jamie clutching her arm for support. "It's all right, dearie; Frank ain't mixed up in it."

They saw him coming down the street then, hurrying. As Kinnard bent down over the wounded man, Jamie heard someone step out on the veranda behind them. With a gasp of horror she saw it was Steve Portugay.

"Frank!" she screamed a split second before Steve fired.

The slug clipped Kinnard's ear as he looked up and saw Portugay, and Jamie with Belle—saw all three of them in one glance. With maddening deliberation he stood there and took a second shot from little Steve's gun that slapped his sleeve. He fired then. The impact of the bullet lifted Portugay to his toes. He fell forward and hung there over the veranda railing, grotesque in his last agony.

Jamie tore her eyes away and saw Worth Arnett step out of the photographer's tent, gun raised, his handsome face hate-ridden and hideous. She tried to scream a warning. Her lips parted but terror held her speechless.

Kinnard needed no warning. When he saw he had nothing further to fear from Portugay, he whirled around, certain that if Arnett tried to gun him the attack would not come from that direction. He caught the movement of the tent flap. For a split second that seemed endless, the two of them stared at each other in a frozen glance.

The Texan's expression did not change, but his mind was working swiftly. In that fraction of a second all his long conflict with Kinnard passed in review before his eyes. He realized that the advantage that had been his but a moment ago was gone now, wasted. He damned Portugay for a blundering fool. Suddenly he darted back into the tent. A violent agitation of the canvas followed, threatening to bring the tent down. Jamie's heart missed a beat as she saw Kinnard rush in after him.

Arnett was gone; he had pulled up the back wall and slipped out. Kinnard scrambled after him and saw him disappear around the loading platform at the rear of Powers' store. He snapped a shot at him that sent splinters flying. The platform was too low to offer any real advantage. There was a wagon yard just beyond. As Kinnard ran up, Arnett fired and bolted in among the wagons—freighting outfits and ranch wagons.

"They're back in the wagon yard!" Jamie heard a man shout. Belle felt her sagging against her.

"You want me to get you inside?" she asked, putting her arm around Jamie.

"No—No—I've got to know what happens!"

She winced at every shot that punctuated the grisly game of hide-and-seek Kinnard and Arnett were playing. There would be no getting away this time. Both knew it. Arnett doubled back around a loaded freighter. For the moment, he had lost Kinnard.

"Turn around!" the latter called.

Arnett knew this was it. He turned and fired before he had a target. Kinnard stepped out in the open, twenty feet away. One shot, and it didn't miss. He stood there for what seemed a long time, drawing breath into his constricted lungs and staring at Arnett, stretched out in the dust.

Jamie saw him when he emerged from the opening between the tent and Powers' and promptly fainted. Belle carried her inside and placed her on the bed. She heard someone running up the stairs. She went to the door. It was Kinnard.

"Belle, is she all right?"

"She will be in a minute or two. She fainted after it was all over . . . You got both of them, Frank?"

"Yeh," he nodded woodenly. "I don't know what you were doing here, Belle, but I'm glad you were with her."

"So am I. She measures up, Frank. Don't let her get away from you." She looked at his ear. "You better let me clean you up before she sees you."

He submitted to her ministrations, his attention fixed on Jamie.

"That'll do till you see a doctor," said Belle. "I'll get out of here now; the two of you don't need me."

When Jamie opened her eyes, Kinnard was bending over her.

"You take it easy," he murmured solicitously. "Everything's all right." He placed his hand against her cheek. "I been giving you a bad time, Jamie. Can you forgive me?"

"There's nothing to forgive, darling. Back in Ogalalla I told you that because one of us got a little pig-headed it wasn't any excuse for the other to be pig-headed, too. Remember?"

"I remember," he smiled tenderly. "I aim to keep that in mind, Jamie—"

"Then put your arms around me and kiss me, Frank—I've waited so long."

It wasn't a moment that needed words to find expression. The minutes passed unnoticed until he said:

"You know, Jamie, they've got ministers in this town as well as bankers."

"I know," she whispered. "I'd much rather throw our business to a minister, Frank."

Center Point Large Print
600 Brooks Road / PO Box 1
Thorndike, ME 04986-0001 USA

(207) 568-3717

US & Canada:
1 800 929-9108
www.centerpointlargeprint.com